KYLE'S ISLAND

SALLY DERBY

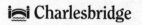 Charlesbridge

With love and pride, I dedicate this, my first novel, to David, my first son, whose love affair with water began at the lake—S. D.

First paperback edition 2014
Copyright © 2010 by Sally Derby
Island photograph copyright © 2010 by Shutterstock.com/Meelis Endla. Rowboat
   and dock photograph copyright © 2010 iStockphoto.com/Jonny Kristoffersson
All rights reserved, including the right of reproduction in whole or in part in any form.
Charlesbridge and colophon are registered trademarks of Charlesbridge Publishing, Inc.

Published by Charlesbridge
85 Main Street
Watertown, MA 02472
(617) 926-0329
www.charlesbridge.com

Library of Congress Cataloging-in-Publication Data
Derby, Sally.
   Kyle's island/Sally Derby.
      p. cm.
   Summary: Kyle, almost thirteen, spends much of the summer yearning to explore
a nearby island, striving to be a good brother, fishing with an elderly neighbor,
and fuming at his parents over their separation that is forcing his mother to sell
the family's cabin on a Michigan lake.
   ISBN 978-1-58089-316-9 (reinforced for library use)
   ISBN 978-1-58089-317-6 (softcover)
   ISBN 978-1-60734-506-0 (ebook)
   ISBN 978-1-60734-183-3 (ebook pdf)
[1. Conduct of life—Fiction. 2. Brothers and sisters—Fiction. 3. Lakes—Fiction.
4. Islands—Fiction. 5. Separation (Psychology)—Fiction. 6. Family life—Michigan—
Fiction. 7. Michigan—Fiction.] I. Title.
PZ7.D4416Kyl 2010
[Fic]—dc22   2009017581

Printed in the United States of America
(hc) 10 9 8 7 6 5 4 3 2 1
(sc) 10 9 8 7 6 5 4 3 2 1

Display type and text type set in Coldsmith and Columbus MT
Printed and bound by Worzalla Publishing Company
   in Stevens Point, Wisconsin, USA
Production supervision by Brian G. Walker
Designed by Martha MacLeod Sikkema

CHAPTER ONE

I JINGLED THE CAR KEYS, tossed them up and caught them, ran my finger over the bumpy silver chain. There's something about having car keys in your hand. All you have to do is slip the key into the ignition, turn it, and you're in charge. Speed, direction, final destination—you get to decide. But you have to be sixteen. Almost thirteen doesn't cut it.

So I couldn't start the car, but I could blow the horn. I did—loud and angry. Mom stuck her head out the front door. "Vicki back?" she asked.

"No, she isn't. And neither is Josh. What's with this family? We were supposed to leave an hour ago."

"A half hour. They'll be here. Is the car all packed?"

She was trying to change the subject, so I ignored the question. "Why don't we call Josh home, and as soon as he gets here, we all wait in the car? Then when Vicki gets dropped off, we can just start up and leave."

Okay, so that was a dumb suggestion, but she could have answered me. Instead she gave me the Look—I think the Look is the first thing teachers learn in college—and went back in. Grumbling to myself, I opened the car door and slid into the driver's seat. I sat there with my eyes closed, imagining I was in one of those new passenger vans instead of our '69 wagon. I shouldn't have had to imagine. Dad always said a car's got only five good years, and then you should trade it in. So, '69 to '74—that's five years, right? But Dad was gone. Long gone. No Dad, no new car. On Valentine's Day—how's that for timing?—he'd kissed Mom and the girls good-bye, hugged Josh and me, and said he hoped he'd be back soon. He had to "think things out." Well, he could think all he wanted. He could stay away forever, as far as I was concerned.

I got out of the wagon, slamming the door behind me, and headed down to the park to get Josh. If Mom wouldn't get things going, I would.

I could hear the voices before I got through the gates: "Here! Here! Pass it!" Josh and a bunch of other six- and seven-year-olds were kicking around soccer balls.

"Hey, Josh! Come on—we gotta leave," I called.

"Already? Can't I play a little more?"

"Come on!"

4

Josh mumbled something to another boy, ran over to grab his ball, and left the field. He walked past me and out the gate, his head down, his arm wrapped around the ball. He didn't look at me.

For a minute I felt bad for him. I knew he didn't want to go to the lake. Where he did want to go was to soccer camp with his friends. But with Dad gone, there was no money for that. So he was sulking. Josh could hold a sulk for a long time. Maybe the whole summer.

"Listen, Josh," I said, catching up with him. "The lake is fun, remember? We'll swim, fish . . ."

"I don't like fishing, and I'm no good at swimming."

"That's only because you won't put your face in the water. Once you learn to do that, you'll be lots better. I'll work with you this summer, teach you some strokes."

"You will?" He looked at me sideways. "Dad was going to teach me. He's a good swimmer."

Another broken promise. "I'm a good swimmer, too," I said. "C'mon, let's run."

As we got home and started up the driveway, the front door opened and Andrea came out on the porch. "Is Vicki back?" I called. "It's time to leave."

"Not yet. But Mom and I are ready."

"About time," I grumbled.

Andrea just grinned. "Don't be a crosspatch, Kyle." She kind of skipped down the steps, a pencil case in her hand and a sketchbook under her arm, as usual. She kept coming until she stood nose-to-nose with me. "Crosspatch, draw the latch, sit by the fire and spin." She recited the old nursery rhyme in a singsongy voice that made me laugh. "That's better," she said. She moved an inch closer. "I'm taller than you today. Isn't that right, Josh?"

Josh checked us out. "Nope, Kyle's still taller," he said.

"It's going to stay like that, too," I told Andrea. "No way you're getting ahead of me again." Andrea and I are twins, but she'd always been a little taller than me. This past Christmas Day, though, we were even, and I passed her up in January.

Just then a car drew up, and Vicki hopped out. "Thanks," she called back over her shoulder. She hurried over to us. "Sorry I'm late, guys. Andrea, wait till you see my suit!"

"How come you waited till today to decide you needed a new one?" I asked. "At least you're here now. Finally, we can leave."

"I just have to go to the bathroom and get my books."

"More books? Why don't you bring the whole library?" I asked. But you can't argue with Vicki, not about books.

6

Not about anything else, either, now that she's fifteen. She just raised an eyebrow and flipped back her hair. "Well, hurry up," I said.

Mom came out as Vicki went in. We might as well have had a revolving door there. Mom beckoned. Now what? It was time to go, darn it. Past time.

"Dad's on the phone," Mom called. Her face was shining the way it always does when she talks about him. "He wants to talk to everyone before we leave. First Kyle."

"Sure he wants to talk to us." I put all the sarcasm I could into my voice. "That's why he's not here. Tell him I'm busy."

"Oh, Kyle. You wouldn't talk last time. I wish you weren't so angry at him."

"I'm not angry. I just don't have anything to say. Are we ever going to leave?"

She didn't push, just turned away and hurried back in. Josh hurried after her. Why should they hurry? If Dad didn't love us enough to stay with us, why should we bother with him? Every time they talked, Mom ended up thinking about him for hours. You could tell. You'd ask her a question, and she'd just say "Hmm?" and not listen. It made me sick. It was a good thing we were going to the lake. Maybe up there she could get him out of her mind.

Andrea told me, "If I wanted to draw a scowl, I'd draw your face right now."

"Is this better?" I pulled down the corners of my mouth and stuck out my tongue. She laughed and made a face back. I gave her a little shove. "Go hurry up Josh. He'll talk to Dad for hours if you let him."

I leaned against the wagon, tossing the keys up and down, up and down.

CHAPTER TWO

FOUR HOURS LATER I HAD counted twenty-eight bug cars and Josh had forty-five. I was still trying to get used to seeing Andrea up in the front seat. I'd planned to sit there, of course, but Vicki said she should because she was the oldest, and Josh said he should because he was the youngest. (I don't know how he thought that made sense.) Then Mom said, "I've already decided. I want Andrea up here with me—she's the one who likes to read maps."

"You don't need a map to get to the same place you've been going every summer for years and years," I pointed out, but Mom said there might be a detour or something, and she'd feel better if Andrea was beside her with the map. I was going to argue, but Mom's voice got a little shaky on the word "detour." I took a quick look at her and saw her left eyelid begin to flutter. It only does that when she's nervous. The way she hates to drive, I figured we'd better get going before she chickened out. "C'mon, Josh, we'll get in the back with Vicki," I said. "We can count bug cars on the way."

"Okay!" His voice was cheerful. He'd known he didn't really have a chance at the front seat. He just likes to argue.

Vicki had climbed in on the driver's side, so I took the middle, letting Josh sit by the window, which was very mature of me. Other years Andrea and I would have had the whole "way back" to sit or lie down in, because our suitcases would be up in the luggage rack. Dad always stowed them up there, along with extra boxes and stuff. He made lifting even Vicki's suitcase full of books look easy. Mom would worry that things would fall off, and then Dad would say, "Are you doubting my prowess, Woman?" That would make her laugh, and start the trip off happy. But this year when we'd gotten all the bags lined up on the curb, she opened the back and said, "In here," like it was no different than usual. But it was.

Mom started the car. Andrea unfolded the map, and Vicki picked up her book. I figured we wouldn't hear anything from her for the rest of the ride, but to my surprise she didn't begin to read right away. "Jen and Tracey are seeing *American Graffiti* at the drive-in tonight," she said. "I'm going to miss so much this summer."

"Yeah—Cincinnati heat and humidity. You'll really miss

those. Are you crazy, Vick? Think of Michigan nights, think of diving off Marshalls' float."

"I suppose so. . . ." She'd opened her book. I looked over at her—what was with her this year? Her long hair hid her face as she bent her head over her reading. Whatever was bugging her, she'd get over it when we got to the cottage.

"Fifty-one!"

"I give."

"Okay. Want to play alphabet?"

"Sure," I said, although I didn't.

Mom actually turned her head away from the road long enough to flash me a smile. "Thank you," she mouthed.

So I played two games of alphabet with Josh, then he talked me into playing tic-tac-toe. Do you know how many tic-tac-toe games you can play driving through Indiana? I lost count around three hundred. (And if you think that's an exaggeration, let me just say that even Josh wasn't heartbroken when the pencil broke and we couldn't find another.)

The ride seemed longer than usual, and no one was in a very good mood, not even me. Other years Dad had kept us all laughing and joking. He's a really good storyteller, even if he is a jerk, and he used to tell these long, involved stories about Isabel and Ike—twins (of course) who lived on a lake and kept getting into trouble in weird and funny ways. The stories made you forget all about being cooped up in a car. When he wasn't telling a story, he was acting the part of tour bus driver, calling out the names of all the little towns we were going through—Churubusco, Ligonier, Dunlap—and making up crazy "points of interest" like "the oldest two-story building in Elkhart County." Andrea did her best, but she doesn't really have a tour-director voice. And when Mom drives, that's all she does, drive— her hands so tight on the steering wheel I'm surprised she doesn't have to be pried loose when the car stops.

In Elkhart we stopped for sandwiches and groceries, and now we had brown paper sacks on our laps and plastic bags at our feet, and the car smelled of apples and cheese. As soon as we crossed the border into Michigan and Cassopolis County, even Josh knew we were close. He started to put away the Matchbox cars he had scattered all over the seat and floor. (I had threatened to throw them out the window if I sat or stepped on another one.)

The narrow road went straight and level like an arrow pointed at the lake. Trees crowded in on either side till it felt like we were driving through a long green tunnel. We rolled down the windows and let the summer air take the place of the air-conditioning. Much better. I forgot about the way Josh was hogging most of the seat and leaned forward to look through the windshield. Pretty soon we would take a curve to the right, and I'd get this summer's first glimpse of the lake.

Suddenly, there it was. It was greenish-gray tonight, with whitecaps as far as you could see. There was just that one glimpse, and then the car was climbing the hill, and a line of cottages blocked the view. The road ran along the backs of the cottages, and in front of them the land sloped steeply down. I saw that the Dieners were here. And the Wilks. Most people I didn't know by name, only by sight from years back. But anyone who was out waved as we went by, and it felt like a homecoming.

We turned the last curve, and there was our cottage, small and gray with red trim around the windows and along the edge of the roof. Over the back door was a wooden sign. "Gladimere," it said. That's what Gram had named it: "Glad I'm here." Lame, I know, but it was like Gram, and it always made me smile when I thought of it. Even though Gram hadn't stayed at the cottage while we were there, we always knew she was just back in Cassopolis. We'd take a couple of days to visit her there, and often she'd drive over to see us. But she'd died in December. For some reason, that made the cottage look lonely. I guess because it was still boarded up from the winter. Other summers, she'd have been out here before us, raising the shutters that were hinged at the top and acted as awnings once they were propped open, and airing out the cottage. Funny, I hadn't thought much about missing her, but suddenly I realized I did.

I climbed over Josh so I'd be the first one out of the car. It felt so good to straighten my legs. I opened the front door and smiled at Andrea, wondering why she hadn't moved. "Hey!" I said. "We're here!"

She kind of wrinkled her eyebrows and gave her head a little jerk toward Mom, who was just sitting there, not moving. "Mom?" I asked. "Mom, you all right?" She turned her head toward me, but she didn't seem to focus exactly. "You made it," I told her. "Another fine job of driving."

That kind of woke her up—it was what she always said to Dad at the end of a trip—and she smiled, but it was a tired smile. Maybe she was thinking of everything we still had to do before we were really settled in. "Well, might as well get started," she said.

We never unloaded right away. First we'd file around the cottage on the pump side and go straight to the flight of steps leading down the hill. From the top you could see the lake stretched out in front of you, with the opposite shore only a blurry line. Nothing but the pier and the water and the island about halfway across. We stood there and looked our fill, then Mom unlocked the padlock on the door of the screened-in porch.

"I get to sleep out here!" Josh called, pushing ahead.

"Mom?" Vicki appealed.

But this time things went my way. "Kyle will sleep on the porch," Mom said as we went on into the main room. "Vicki and Andrea will sleep in the big bed, and Josh can have the roll-away or the upper bunk. I'll take the lower."

"The bunk! I want the bunk!" Josh almost mowed Vicki down on his way to the bunk. He started up the ladder.

"First, we unload," Mom said firmly.

"I'll prime the pump," Vicki offered. I should have been quicker. I like to be the one who primes the pump. The cottage had no indoor plumbing, just the outhouse down the hill—and the less said about that, the better—but the water from the pump is the best-tasting water there is.

"Guess we'd better get busy," Andrea said, smiling at me. She grabbed Josh by the waistband of his jeans and pulled him off the ladder. Then the three of us went out to the car while Mom started setting things up in the kitchen. It wasn't long till I smelled coffee. For some reason, smelling the coffee made me feel almost like crying. Dumb. But in my memory the blue pot on the stove at the lake is always perking, and the cottage is always filled with the

15

smell of coffee. I don't know how something that tastes so bad can smell so good.

It took us a couple of hours to get the car unloaded, the beds made up, and the suitcases stowed away under the beds. By then it was way dark, and Josh was so tired he climbed straight up the ladder to his bunk, with his copy of *Billy and Blaze* under his arm. I'll bet he didn't read two pages before he went to sleep. Andrea and Mom were sitting at the kitchen table talking, and Vicki was lying across her bed reading (what else?), so I let myself quietly out the front door and went down to the lake. As I walked along the pier, I smiled at the hollow, drumlike sound of my footsteps on the slats. By the benches at the end, I stopped and looked up at the night sky.

There are a million stars in the sky above the lake that you never see in Cincinnati. The moon was out, and its light lay on the water like a stream of spilled milk. Crickets chirped. An owl hooted. A damp breeze lifted the hair hanging down to my collar, and I was glad I was letting it grow. I pulled my jacket close. I stood looking out at the water, at the shadowy mound of the island, at the lights on the opposite shore. It was so beautiful. A tight knot in my chest that I didn't know I'd had just sort of melted away. "We're back," I whispered to the lake. Then I sat down on one of the benches and stretched my legs out and tilted my head back to look up at the sky. I was as happy at that minute as I had been for months. At least this part of my world, the lake, the cottage, hadn't changed, wouldn't change, I thought. Life up here would go on the same as always.

CHAPTER THREE

I WOKE TO THE SOUND OF hammering nearby. Cripes, it wasn't even full light yet. Who was working at this hour? The hammering stopped, then started again, a little farther away, and I realized—a woodpecker, that's what it was! I'd forgotten how loud woodpeckers can be. I didn't mind, though. Thanks to him or her, I'd get an early start on the day. Now I heard other birds stirring and chirping, and the light beyond the screens seemed to brighten by the minute. I lay under the warm covers a bit more, then stretched my arms over my head. Right away goose bumps puckered my skin. I could feel a smile stretch across my face. I threw the blankets off and jumped to my feet, pulling my jeans on in a hurry. Sweatshirt and sneakers, and I was ready to go.

I opened the door to the cottage proper. It was warmer in here, dark and still except for quiet whispers of breath. I tiptoed through to the kitchen, opened the fridge, and grabbed the milk carton. I raised the carton to my lips and took long gulps. Naturally I couldn't do that when Mom was around, but I figured, why dirty a glass—washing dishes up here was a real production. You had to pump a teakettle of water, carry it inside to heat on the stove, pour a pan for washing and a pan for rinsing . . . you get the idea. I put the milk carton back, grabbed an envelope of Pop-Tarts, and went out into the morning, careful not to let the screen door slam. At the pump I splashed cold water on my face. My toothbrush, along with everyone else's, was waiting in the cup on the shelf outside the door. But I didn't see any point in brushing if I was going to eat Pop-Tarts in a minute, so I just swished some water around in my mouth, then hurried down to the lake.

The reeds to the west were still wrapped in mist, and the Wilks' sailboat, bobbing at anchor a few cottages down, was only a ghostly shape. From the fields behind the cottages a crow cawed, and another answered from farther away. I took off my sneakers and rolled up my jeans, got the oars and life jackets from the shed, and laid them on the pier. Then I dragged the rowboat down to the lake, which wasn't easy, believe me. I was sweating by the time I got the boat into the water. I gave it a strong shove, then jumped in after it. The shallow water felt warm on my legs, compared to the chilly air, and the bottom was squishy under my feet. I tied the boat to the pole sticking out of the water, then waded to shore, watching out for clamshells—they weren't sharp enough to cut, but it hurt to step on them. Back on the pier, I maneuvered the oars down into the boat and buckled on my life jacket. Then I stepped into the boat, untied the rope, and pushed off.

This was the second summer I was allowed out in the boat by myself. First I'd had to pass a zillion swim lessons at the Y, and then I'd had to promise faithfully never to fish without my life jacket. And still Mom hadn't wanted to say yes. I remembered standing at the cottage door last June and seeing Dad put his arm around her. "Let him go, Dorrie," he'd said. "He's sensible and careful, and you've got to let go sometime."

She'd given him a long, funny look, and I kind of held my breath until she shook her head a little and smiled. "Go on, then," she told me. "I can't hold out against both of you." And Dad had walked down the steps with me and handed me my bait can, then stood on the pier watching as I rowed away.

Today it took me just a few minutes to row past the end of the pier and head toward the island. Later on I would get bait, and Josh and I would fish. Right now I just wanted to enjoy being almost alone on the lake. It was "almost," because out beyond the point of the island the serious bluegill and bass fishermen were already hunched over their poles. The water was deep there; they wouldn't be disturbed by small fish nibbling at their bait. When a fish took the bait, pulling the bobber under with an I-mean-business downward tug, a cry of "Socko!" would go up, and the other fishermen would glance over with brief interest.

I rowed steadily, watching the cottages on the hill grow smaller as I got farther from shore. When I was about fifty feet from the island, I turned the boat and let it drift while I studied the tree- and bush-covered shoreline. This was the year, I promised myself. This summer I was finally going to explore the island. By myself. Dad had said it was uninhabited, except by birds and maybe a snake or two, but I wanted to investigate anyway. It wasn't a large island, only about the size of a football field, and it rose from the water in a gentle mound like the back of a giant turtle. Did that border of crowded trees and bushes extend clear to the other side? Maybe someplace in there was a clearing or two you couldn't see from the water. Maybe there was a cave. Could you have a cave on an island? Sometimes I was sure I could see the trace of a path leading into the trees from a point on the southwestern tip, but Dad had said I was imagining it. Well, I wasn't taking his word for anything anymore. I'd find out for myself if he was right about the island. Soon.

After I'd rowed around the island, I headed back toward the cottage. I thought it would be nice to put on a pot of coffee for Mom while she was still asleep. But when I climbed the steps, I found her sitting on the bottom of the two steps to the porch. A cup of coffee sat on the step beside her, and she was smoking a cigarette. That was Dad's fault. She'd quit years ago, but the day after Valentine's she'd gone out and bought a pack of cigarettes, and she'd come home and lit one in front of all of us with a look that just dared us to complain. None of us said a word, but I'd seen tears in Andrea's eyes.

"Been out around the island?" Mom asked me now.

"Yeah."

"We'll get some bait this morning."

"I know."

I sat down beside her, and we just stayed there listening to the birds and the sound of the water lapping the rocks along the shore until the door behind us creaked open and Josh threw his arms around Mom's neck and twisted around into her lap. "Brrrr. Keep me warm," he said.

That was the end of the quiet time. Mom fixed breakfast while Andrea played catch with Josh down by the lake and Vicki folded up the roll-away bed. "I thought you and Andrea were going to share the big bed," I said.

"Sleeping with Andrea is like sharing a lifeboat with a puppy," Vicki said grumpily. "It's no wonder she's so skinny—she doesn't lie still for two minutes straight. She turns, and she shifts, and the springs creak, and the mattress moves up and down constantly. It's enough to make you seasick, so I pulled out the roll-away. I don't see why I can't have the porch. You've got a reading lamp and everything. Just because . . ."

She was winding up for her Just Because You're a Boy speech when we heard Mom's warning—"Victoria!" She was quiet then, but she threw a dirty look at the kitchen doorway. Vicki doesn't wake up well. At home she'd sleep until eleven, but even she couldn't sleep with four other people moving around in three small rooms.

I went into the kitchen to start making toast, and Vicki went outside. "I'm going to take a little walk down the road," she called through the screen door. In just a bit she came back with a handful of purple flowers she put in a glass on the middle of the table.

Andrea came up from the lake just then. "How pretty!" she said when she saw the flowers.

"Aren't they?" Vicki answered. "Hey, maybe you could begin with them!" She and Andrea exchanged what a book would call a "significant" look. It bugged me a little—what could be significant about a handful of flowers?

"Begin what?" I asked, but Vicki said only, "Oh, just an idea Andrea and I had last night. Nothing important." She paused. "We'll have to throw them out if they make me sneeze, though," she went on. "I don't know why I have to have hay fever when none of the rest of you do."

Just then Mom brought over bacon and eggs, so we dug in and began to make plans for the day. We had plenty of time to plan, because we all ate a lot. Food tastes really good at the lake, even things you don't ordinarily like. I don't know why that is.

We'd cleared the plates when Mom brought over a box of glazed doughnuts. "Dessert?" she asked with a smile. While we ate the doughnuts, we made a list of things for Mom to get from the little store on the way to Cassopolis. I asked, "Who's going to go with you?"

"I'm going by myself," she answered. "I've a couple of things to do that won't be interesting to any of you. Victoria, if you'll watch Josh very carefully while I'm gone, I'll see that you have time to sunbathe and read this afternoon. Andrea and Kyle will clean up the kitchen, then check to

24

make sure the fishing poles are ready to use. I won't be gone more than an hour or two."

"An hour or two!" I said. "You can't spend an hour or two at that little store. Not even picking out bait and getting your fishing license."

"I'm going on into Cassopolis," Mom said. "I told you I had a couple of things to attend to."

Mom had a lot of business details to look after when Gram died. She was an only child, so she had to close all Gram's accounts and pay her bills and things like that. Maybe she had more of that stuff to do. Still, an hour or two! I probably wouldn't get to fish before lunch, and after lunch was the worst time of day for fishing. I might as well wait until suppertime. "Cripes," I muttered. Mom gave me the Look, but I ignored it. "Why can't—"

"Hey, Kyle, look sharp!" I raised my head when I heard Dad's old phrase, and my hand shot up to grab the half-doughnut flying toward me.

"Andrea!" Mom protested.

"I can't eat any more," Andrea said, sort of fake-innocently.

"That's not the point and you know it." Mom was glaring, but her lips were twitching.

"Thanks, Andy," I said, smiling. Andrea the peacemaker, at it again.

"No problem." She smiled back at me, and for the millionth time I thought how much I like being a twin.

When Mom came back from Cassopolis, her eyes were red and her face was kind of blotchy-looking. I'd thought she was over grieving for Gram, but I guess it takes a long time to quit missing your mother. I don't even like to think about things like that. Anyway, she looked so unhappy I didn't complain when I found out she'd forgotten to buy the bait.

"That's okay, I can walk down to Clyde's," I told her. "Or I can just go dig some worms across the road."

"Not until I've asked the Dieners if it's still okay for you to dig there. I suppose it is, but it won't hurt to check. Besides, Clyde will be glad to see you."

Clyde's Bait Shop was just down the road half a mile or so. He was a nice guy, and his prices were fair, but we never bought bait after the first day. By the time it was gone, I'd have dug enough red worms and found enough night crawlers to keep us supplied. I even caught crickets sometimes and put them in Gram's old cricket cage, but I didn't like using them. I wouldn't tell everyone, but I have kind of a soft spot for crickets. It seems a shame to drown that pretty song.

The road to Clyde's is the one that runs along the backs of the cottages, the same one you come in on. It goes all around the lake, I think, but we'd never driven down the other way. Once you got to the lake, the last thing you wanted to do was get into a car and leave, even for a little while.

Walking along the road, kicking at stones and watching the dust cloud around my sneakers, I let my ears fill with peacefulness. The birds were quieter than they'd been earlier, and there was no breeze. Now and then you'd hear a screen door slam, and sometimes you could hear voices from down at the water's edge, but mostly it was so quiet I felt as if I were the only one around.

When I got to Clyde's and stepped inside, it took my eyes a few seconds to adjust to the dimness of the shop. There were only two people there—Clyde, and Tom Butler. The shop wasn't much, just one room, with an old cash register on a countertop, some shelves, a couple stools, and two refrigerators. One refrigerator was for bait, and one was for beer and soft drinks. For such a little place, it was amazing how Clyde's shelves always seemed to hold what you needed, from candles and fuses to playing cards and dish towels.

"Afternoon," said Clyde when I came in. "Kyle Chester, isn't it?"

"Yes, sir," I said. "Afternoon. Afternoon, Mr. Butler."

"Sorry about your grandmother, Kyle," Clyde told me. "We all miss Hazel Cook. I thought she was one of those who'd go on forever. Well, you never can tell."

"Thank you." That seemed a funny answer when someone said they missed your gram, but I couldn't think what else to say.

"You here for the summer?"

"I hope so. Mom won't say for sure how long we're staying. The longer the better for me."

"What's your dad say?"

"Dad's not with us. I'd like a pint of red worms," I added in a hurry, hoping to avoid any more questions about Dad.

Clyde seemed to take the hint—at least he moved over to the refrigerator and took out an old dirt-filled cottage cheese carton. He came back and plopped it on the countertop. "Lucky you came early," he told me. "I'm having trouble keeping up with the demand these days. You dig your own worms most of the time, don't you?"

"Yeah, back behind the cottage the soil's full of them."

"Well, if you want to make some spending money, I'll be glad to buy some off you. Whatever you can provide. Boy who used to supply me is off to college this year, and his younger brother's as lazy as an old sow."

"That'd be great," I said. "I could use a little money."

Tom Butler spoke up then. "Tell your momma I said hello, will you?" It must have been the first time in my life I ever heard Tom Butler speak. He was known for his silence, and if I'd ever heard his voice before, I sure would have remembered it. It was an announcer's voice, deep and kind of husky.

It was hard not to stare at him. He was the fattest man I'd ever seen. Not just fat, enormous. The pouches of fat under his jaws made whatever neck he had disappear. His stomach bulged out over his thighs. Even his hands were fat—his wedding ring cut into his finger like a rubber band wound around once too often. It was kind of disgusting. It wasn't a Santa Claus kind of fat; there was too much of him for that. But his eyes were Santa Claus eyes. Blue, and crinkly around the edges.

"Yes, sir, Mr. Butler, I'll tell her," I said.

I paid for my red worms and started to go, but then Clyde opened the door to the second refrigerator. "Here, have one on me," he said, handing me a bottle of root beer. "In honor of our new partnership."

"Thanks," I said. I started back to the cottage all light-footed and excited. I wondered how much I could earn selling red worms. Anything would help, I thought. Mom didn't talk a lot about money, but I had noticed the worry on her face whenever she went through the mail, pulling out the bills. I suppose by the time she paid the mortgage and bought food and stuff, there wasn't much of her paycheck left. It wasn't as if we'd had a lot extra even when Dad was with us. Schoolteachers, which is what Mom and Dad are, don't earn very much money. What made him think it was fair to have an apartment all to himself? I'll bet his rent cost him more than Josh's soccer camp would have.

There I went—Dad again. Think of something else, I scolded myself. I began planning the afternoon. As soon as I got back, I'd change into my swim trunks and start coaching Josh a little.

I was almost at the cottage when I noticed it. A sign, stuck in the dirt of our parking space. What was a sign doing there? I drew closer, close enough to read the writing. "For Sale," it said. "Dave Becker Realty." And it had a telephone number and a Cassopolis address below that.

Somebody had made a mistake. I'd better tell Mom. She'd want it moved right away. I ran into the cottage and set my bait carton on the kitchen table. Where was she? I found her on the porch in the old wicker rocker. "Mom?" I asked.

She turned her face to me. "Back already?" She smiled,

but there was something wrong with her smile. I didn't take time to try figuring it out.

"Mom, some dope's put a For Sale sign by our cottage. It's out in back. You better tell the real estate people to move it—their telephone number's on the sign."

"A sign?" she said. "Dave's already put up a sign? Damn." I saw the pity in her face then, and I knew. I knew before she said another word. "I'm sorry, Kyle. I was sitting here trying to think how to tell you. I didn't know Dave had put a sign up. You shouldn't have found out this way."

CHAPTER FOUR

SO IT WAS TRUE. I STARED at her, and she stared back.
I went through the doorway, sat down on the footstool in
front of her. "You're selling the cottage?" I could hear my
voice getting louder. "Gram's cottage? Our cottage? The first
year it's all ours and you're selling it?"

"I am." Mom's voice trembled, but I'd heard that tone
before. There was steel in it.

"Why?" I didn't think I was shouting, but maybe I was,
because Mom flinched.

"We can't afford to keep it, Kyle. The taxes alone are
eight hundred dollars a year. And there's upkeep. When
Mom was up here, she could keep an eye on things, hire
someone to put the pier in and out, lime the outhouse, cut
down weeds. . . . You can't manage a property when you're
two hundred miles away." I didn't want to listen. I tried to

answer, but she didn't give me a chance to say anything. She just plowed ahead. "Besides," she said, "The money we'll get from the sale can go into the college fund. That's always been a worry, how we could afford to send all of you, and now that your dad—" she broke off, swallowed, began again. "Vicki's already a sophomore, and when you and Andrea go, too . . ."

"Forget about college—I'm not going."

That stopped her. "Not going to college? Oh, Kyle, of course you are. These days . . ."

"Not if we have to sell the cottage to get the money, I'm not. And I'll bet Vicki and Andrea won't go either. Where are they? Do they know?"

"I told them just before you got back. Do you know what Andrea said? 'Poor Kyle.' She knew, we all knew how hard this would be for you. And I was planning how— darn Dave!"

"What did Vicki say, and Josh?" I asked bitterly. "I'll bet they're glad. They didn't want to come anyway."

"They aren't glad." Mom pulled a cigarette out of the pack beside her on the table. "They're sorry, too. We're all sorry, Kyle."

"Sorry doesn't help. Why don't you do something?" I

stood up so fast my elbow knocked against the big flash-light we kept on the table for trips down the hill at night. It banged to the floor, but I didn't bother to pick it up.

"There's nothing I can do." Mom said that so quietly I could hardly hear, and for some reason that made me an-grier than ever.

"There's gotta be something! You give up too easy." I was shouting again.

"Kyle, if you'll just look at this reasonably—"

"The hell with reason!" My voice bounced off the cot-tage walls. "First you can't hold on to Dad, and now you want to take the cottage away from us. This stinks!"

Mom didn't answer. Her hand flew up to her cheek, like I'd hit her. For a moment I was sorry, then I wasn't sorry at all. She wouldn't fight for anything, not the cottage, not Dad. She'd just let Dad leave, let him have everything his way. I'd heard her tell him he could come back whenever he wanted. She'd be waiting, she said. But maybe he'd never want to, maybe he'd want a divorce instead. Had she thought of that?

I had to get out of there. I was a time bomb ready to explode. She had no idea. I wanted to throw something, hit something or someone, run until I dropped. I moved back from her, stumbling a little. My foot bumped against the flashlight, and I kicked it, hard. It spun crazily across the room, hit the opposite wall. I had my hand on the door when Mom's voice stopped me. "I couldn't help what happened with your father, Kyle. And I can't help this. Regardless of what you think."

I went out then. I let the screen door bang behind me.

* * *

Down by the lake I saw Vicki, Andrea, and Josh just sitting on the pier, dangling their legs over the side. Andrea's head turned when the door banged. She waved for me to come down, then said something to Vicki. Vicki moved over and patted the place where she'd been sitting, like she was coaxing some little kid. Well, I was coming, wasn't I?

"Are you okay?" Andrea asked as soon as I came near.

It took me a minute to get calm enough to answer. "Mad, that's all," I muttered.

"We heard you yell," Josh said. "Kids aren't supposed to yell at grown-ups."

Just what I needed: a lecture from my little brother. I took a deep breath, all set to blast him, but then I saw the way he was looking at me. He looked so sad—pathetic, really. I shut my mouth. Josh sat there between the girls, soccer ball beside him like always, fooling with a clamshell. He didn't look at me again.

"I'm sorry about the yelling," I said. "Don't worry—things will work out somehow. We're staying right here in the cottage, the way we planned. If anyone wants to buy it, they'll have to buy us, too."

"Can they do that?" He sounded really alarmed.

I laughed. We all laughed. After a minute, Josh did, too. It was like laughing was something we needed right then. Josh handed me the clamshell. "I'm going to start a collection of lake treasures right away, so I'll always have them," he said. "This shell is my first. Do you want me to find one for you, too? There are lots."

I held the shell so tight its sharp edge dug into my palm. I felt like throwing the dumb thing into the water. I didn't want a treasure collection. I wanted the cottage. But when I looked at Josh's face, I could tell he really wanted to make me feel better. "That's a great idea," I told him. He can be a good kid sometimes.

He jumped down into the water and started wading around, bending over every so often to run his hands along the mucky bottom. I sat down in his place, and Vicki scooted over to make a little more room for me. "I'm sorry, Kyle," she said. For once, she didn't have a book open. She'd taken off her glasses, too. Without them she looked a little like Mom. "I really am," she went on. "We all know how much you like it here." Andrea had been quiet, just looking at me. Now she said, "You don't look as bad as I thought you would. More mad than sad."

"You're damn—" I noticed Josh look over at me and corrected myself. "Darn right I'm mad. It was going to be so good, coming up here—now it's like someone gives you this great birthday present and then takes it away two seconds later. Why did she even bother bringing us up here? Just so she could sell it?"

"Maybe she wanted us to have this one last time. We are here, Kyle. And maybe it won't happen—maybe no one will want to buy it. Don't let this spoil the time we have."

"It's already spoiled." But as usual, Andrea had made me feel kind of better. Ever since we were little kids, she's always known how to do that.

As we all sat together on the pier, I stared out at the island. One thing was for sure—this summer I was going to get on that island, explore it properly. I wondered how much time we had.

"Someone's coming to look at the cottage tomorrow," Vicki said, as if in answer to my thoughts. "The Realtor called Mom at the Morleys'." We didn't have a telephone at the cottage, but the Morleys, in the cottage next door, did. They'd always taken any calls for us and let us use their phone if we had to call out. In return we let them use our pier any time they wanted. They were nice people, but they were pretty old. Mr. Morley still fished a little, but his wife hardly ever came outside.

"Kyle, you want to kick the soccer ball for a while?" Josh called to me.

"Just a minute, Josh. Somebody's coming to look at it already?"

"Mmm-hmm. So Mom said we have to be sure our suits and wet towels don't get left on the floor."

"Huh," I scoffed, getting to my feet. "I'm not going to clean the cottage for anybody. They can just see it as it is." Josh climbed back up on the pier and looked at me hopefully. I grabbed him around the neck and gave his head a Dutch rub with my knuckles. He hunched his shoulders and squealed, and I remembered how I used to feel when Dad did that to me—kind of safe and scared at the same time. "Okay, Josh," I said, letting him go, "we'll kick the ball around a bit."

"We'll play, too." Andrea held out her hand to Vicki. Vicki looked uncertain, then laughed and said, "Okay, Andrea and I against Kyle and Josh. Losers do the dishes."

It's funny how sometimes a silly game you've played a thousand times turns into something special. That's the way it was that day. It was like I was playing, but I was watching at the same time. I saw the determined way Josh clenched his jaws when he was dribbling the ball. I saw Vicki's long blond hair kind of floating behind her as she took the ball toward our goal. I saw the tiny beads of sweat on Andrea's upper lip as she tried to dribble past me. I even saw the scab on my knee as I passed the ball to Josh. Our voices seemed to float out over the water. The day was so beautiful, and things were so right between us all.

It's not like this at home, I thought. At home we're all separate and busy, each of us going our own way. Here we're together. Close. We can't lose all this just because of a little money. Why can't Mom see that?

CHAPTER FIVE

I'D SAID I WOULDN'T HELP clean the cottage for the people coming to look at it, but there I was the next morning, sweeping the porch floor with Gram's old straw broom. I hate sweeping. I'd offered to do dishes, but Vicki said she and Andrea were planning to do them, that they had things to talk about. I wasn't sure what to make of that. Josh had volunteered to help Mom make beds, so I could complain or sweep, and I didn't think it was a good day for complaining.

I was still mad at Mom, but a little ashamed, too. You shouldn't let go that way, shouting and all. When I was little and lost my temper, Dad taught me a trick. He said, "You never see me lose my temper, do you, Kyle? You can control your temper or let it control you." And then he'd ask, "Who's boss, son, you or Old Man Temper?" OMT— funny, I hadn't thought of him in years—but it got so all

Dad had to do was grin and say "OMT," and I'd make myself calm down.

Well, yesterday afternoon OMT had sure shown up again. After Josh and I won the soccer game, he'd run up to the cottage to brag to Mom. When he came back down, he looked at me kind of accusingly and said, "Mom's been crying." That wasn't exactly my fault, but no one likes their mom to cry. So today I was being Pleasant and Helpful, the way Mom wanted—up to a point.

"As soon as they get here, we'll pile into the car and go into Elkhart for lunch," Mom told me when I started sweeping in the main room.

I stopped sweeping. "Not me. I want to stay here."

"It would be awkward, Kyle. They'll need privacy to talk to Dave, say what they really think."

"But I won't be where I can hear them. I'll be down by the lake. C'mon, Mom—let me stay." Just in case, I thought. If this really was our last summer here, I didn't want to miss a minute.

Andrea came in from the kitchen, dish towel in one hand, plate in the other. "Lunch will be a lot cheaper without Kyle, Mom—more room in the car that way, too." She winked at me.

"You promise you'll keep out of their way?" Mom

41

sounded doubtful, so I gave her my best smile and put my arm around her shoulders.

"I promise," I said. She shook her head a little then, but she said okay. So around eleven-thirty, when a car pulled up out back, we all went outside.

The Realtor, a tired-looking man in khakis and a blue shirt, was opening the car doors for the couple inside. "Morning, Dorrie," he said to Mom. "Beautiful day, isn't it? I'd like you to meet the Thompsons, Terri and Keith."

"Morning, Dave," Mom said. She held out her hand, and the Thompsons shook it.

"Are you going to buy our cottage?" Josh asked.

The adults all laughed, and Josh scowled and kicked at the dirt. I didn't blame him. Why do grown-ups think it's funny when kids ask what everyone's thinking anyway?

"Kyle's going to stay here, down by the lake," Mom said. "But the rest of us are going into Elkhart. Take as long as you need."

"Thanks, Dorrie," said the Realtor. He led the way into the cottage, and I wondered how the Thompsons would like it. They didn't look like fishermen. They didn't look like cottage people, even. She was dressed up in high heels and a blue pantsuit, and he had cowboy boots on. "C'mon, kids, let's go," Mom said. "You be good now, Kyle."

"Can't I stay with Kyle?" Josh begged for what must have been the millionth time.

"No, we're going," Mom said firmly, and they did.

I started down the steps to the lake. Halfway down I saw movement out of the corner of my eye, something disturbing the sparse ground cover on the hill. I stood still. Sure enough, there it was again—a trembling of leaves right beside the next step down. Then I saw it: a little brown toad, half-hidden by a weed. I bent down slowly. He didn't move. My hand shot out, and I had him. I cupped him in my palm and looked at him. He squatted there, just tickling the skin a bit. He was all angles and bright eyes. I rubbed my thumb down the skin on his back. It was dry and bumpy.

"Wait till Josh sees him," I said. "I've gotta find something to keep him in." A coffee can would work. I could punch holes in the lid and put in grass to make him comfortable. I started back up to the cottage. The murmur of voices came through the screens. It wouldn't hurt if I just slipped into the kitchen for a minute, would it? I went around to the side door and opened it quietly with my free hand. It wasn't easy getting into the fridge and pulling out the can with just one hand, but I managed. Then I was stuck. I needed both hands to pour the coffee into a bowl or something. What could I use . . . ? Sure, why not? I set the can on the counter of the old kitchen cabinet, opened the silverware drawer, popped the toad in and shoved the drawer shut. He should be safe there for a minute. I was poking holes in the can lid when a screech of laughter startled me.

There were open windows between the kitchen and the screened porch. I moved closer to the window. "Well, I realize it's not exactly what you want, but . . . ," Dave the Realtor was saying.

"Not exactly?" Terri Thompson's voice was shrill. "It's impossible. What makes them think anyone will buy a dump like this?"

"It's a fishing cottage, not a resort, Ter," said her husband.

"Yeah, I know, but look at it. No running water, no commode. It doesn't even have any real walls!"

It was a strange way to put it, but I knew what she meant. The cottage was just a shell. There were no plastered walls, no wall board, just the outside walls. To separate the kitchen from the main room, a partition rose partway up, about ceiling height, but there was no ceiling, just a space between the rafters and the inside of the roof. Lots of neat stuff was stored up there on the rafters—spare cane poles and nets, extra chairs, straw hats and boots. A nail on the inside of the back door held Gram's raincoat and a big old denim jacket that had belonged to my grandfather.

"They haven't even painted it inside," Terri was saying. "They write on the walls!" I rolled my eyes when she said that. The writing was one of the things I loved about the cottage. On the partition wall people wrote messages to Gram. "Claude and Lucille, 1938, eleven bass, thirty bluegills." Things like that. Years and years of family history. There was a message from us for each year we'd been here. Of course, if you weren't family, I guess you wouldn't be interested. She sure wasn't.

"You can see this isn't quite what we had in mind," Keith said. "The only thing right is the price, and even at that price I'd expected a little more."

"Lakefront property is hard to come by," Dave Becker pointed out. "And more expensive than you maybe realized. But I've got a couple other places to show you."

I heard footsteps then, and I relaxed. I thought they'd go out the front. They didn't. Just as I reached for the can, the Realtor appeared in the doorway to the kitchen. "Oh, hi there, Kyle," he said. "Didn't know you were in here."

"I was just—" I began, but Terri Thompson pushed past him.

"This place isn't what we want," she told me, "but tell your mom if she ever wants to sell that cabinet, I might be interested." Tap-tapping across the kitchen, she said, "I just want to make sure the drawers are dove-tailed," and before I could stop her, she yanked open the silverware drawer.

The toad jumped. She screamed. He hopped to the floor. She ran for the nearest chair and clambered up, high heels and all. "Get him! Get him!" she yelled. "Oh my God! Oh my God!" I'll bet they could hear her on the other side of the lake. She was sure scaring the toad.

Then Dave and I were crawling around on the floor, while Keith Thompson kept saying, "There he is—no, there. Oh, you just missed him!" like he was giving the commentary at a ball game. Over our heads Terri's screams rose and fell like a siren. It took forever before we caught him, but when I finally had him back in the can, Mr. Thompson had the lid ready and snapped it on.

"You can come down now," he told his wife.

She looked at the open drawer suspiciously. "You don't have any more in there, do you?" she asked.

They left in a hurry then. I stayed where I was until I heard them get into their car and drive away. "All right!" I cheered. "That's one couple who won't be buying the cottage!" I picked up the toad can. "Good job, buddy," I told him. "They were jerks—come here and look down their noses—what did they expect?"

I thought about that as I went outside. The cottage was well-built. It was comfortable. Who wanted a fancy place you'd have to always be cleaning and dusting? A cottage was supposed to be a cottage, not a house.

Toad can in hand, I took the steps in happy jumps. At the bottom, after I'd opened the lid and dropped in some grass and weeds, I put the can in the shade. Then I went down to the pier. I checked on my fish in the live-box. I'd caught seven nice perch before breakfast this morning. I'd clean them later that afternoon, and Mom would fry them for dinner.

Closing the lid of the live-box, I lay down on the hot boards of the pier, put an arm over my eyes to shade them from the sun, and began to make plans. No way was I going to let us lose the cottage. We'd been lucky with the Thompsons. We might not be so lucky next time. Taxes were what I had to think about. If we could get the money for taxes— at least the half due this fall—I could probably persuade Mom not to worry about the college fund for a while.

Maybe Dad could pay them. He loved the lake, loved the cottage. Did he even know Mom planned to sell? Maybe I should write and tell him. But what would I say? And how would I begin? Not "Dear Dad," for sure. Maybe,

"Hi, butthole." I grinned. I'd get in trouble, using language like that. But it'd sure get his attention.

Forget it—I wasn't going to write. It would serve him right if we did lose the cottage. He probably wouldn't care anyway.

And maybe something else would turn up. We could save money—stop going to movies, not order in pizza. Somehow, we would work it out.

I must have dozed a little bit, because I woke when I heard the doors of the wagon slam. Josh came running around the cottage, down the hill. He was moving so fast he almost fell near the bottom, but he caught himself. "Did they buy it?" he asked me.

I smiled up at him. "Nope," I said. "And I don't think they're going to, either." I got to my feet. "Come see what I've got for you."

Josh was as excited about the toad as I knew he would be, even when I told him he could only keep it for the afternoon. I don't believe in keeping wild things for pets. I know how I'd feel if someone tried to pen me up. I don't even like going to the zoo, really. Andrea's like me that way. Except she's worse. She won't even fish.

"Couldn't I keep him just till tomorrow?" Josh begged.

I thought about it. "No," I said finally, "and I'll tell you why. I'll need the coffee can for tonight. I'm going to go night-crawler hunting."

"Can I go too?"

"I guess. If Mom'll let you stay up that late."

"Whoopee!" Josh was off and running up the steps, searching for Mom.

Before I followed him, I turned and looked back at the island. We'd been here three days, and I hadn't been on the island yet. I'd rowed around it every morning, my eyes searching for the most likely place to push through the barrier of trees hiding the interior. It didn't look very hospitable. But that wasn't going to stop me. As soon as I had a whole day to myself, I'd be there.

CHAPTER SIX

IT WAS AFTER TEN THAT NIGHT before I figured it was dark enough to go out. I closed my book and shook Josh's shoulder. He'd fallen asleep right after supper. If he didn't wake easily, I was going to let him sleep. But he was awake in an instant. He wanted to go right out, and I had a tough time convincing him that he had to bundle up and put mosquito repellent on first. "Why do I have to wear a jacket?" he complained. "It's summer."

"Go out on the porch for a minute and you'll see. It gets chilly here when the sun goes down. Besides, a jacket will help against the mosquitoes. They're fierce down by the water."

I guess my tone convinced him, because he didn't do any more grumbling. We went out the kitchen door, past Mom and Andrea and Vicki, who were playing five hundred rummy at the kitchen table. "Not too long, now," Mom said.

"We won't be."

We didn't turn on the spotlight at the bottom of the hill, just used the flashlight to guide our footsteps. There was another toad right next to the steps—at least I thought it was another toad. Josh was sure it was "his," the one he'd turned loose right before supper. "I know it's Freddy. I can tell by his eyes," he said. "See how big they are?"

"All toads have big eyes," I said. For a minute after I said that, I was afraid he was going to cry. I felt bad, but I have to help him grow up—since Dad's not here to do it.

When we stepped onto the grass at the bottom of the hill, I told Josh, "Walk gently. They can feel the vibrations if you step down heavy." I directed the flashlight beam into the grass. "Don't look right at the center of the beam. They hide from the light, and you won't find any there. Look at the shadows around the edge of the circle."

It was only a minute or two before I saw one, and I held the flashlight steady while I knelt down and reached out to grab the worm. "You can't pull too hard or you'll tear it in half," I explained. "But you have to pull some, because they'll try to slide back down into their holes." I pulled gently. "Got him!" I said. "You can get the next one."

Josh turned out to be good at it. Maybe because he's closer to the ground, he seemed to spot them before I did.

We got about twenty, and then I thought we should go back inside. But he wanted to keep hunting, so I let him hold the flashlight and keep on while I walked down to the shore.

I love the lake at night. The water is black and mysterious-looking. It seems almost solid in the dark, like you could walk on it. The waves are quieter than in the daytime. They brush against the rocks along the shore with little kissing sounds. I just stood there a while, wondering what it would be like to be on the island at night. Kind of scary maybe. Did it have any animals? I knew there was an owl. I could hear him sometimes. I could hardly wait to get out there. Josh was too little to go along—he should wait until he's my age—but I could bring something back for him. Maybe one of the turtles that sunned on the fallen tree along the south shore.

A mosquito hummed around my face, and I slapped at it. I remembered I'd promised Mom I wouldn't keep Josh out too late. "C'mon, Josh. That's all for tonight!"

I expected an argument, because he can be kind of bratty sometimes, but he came running over with the coffee can. "I caught seven by myself, Kyle. Big ones! Wait till I tell Vicki! I'll bet she wouldn't even touch one, would she?"

"You won't believe this, but Vicki's an old hand with worms," I answered. "Dad taught her to bait her own hook a long time ago. He told her no self-respecting fisherman would make someone else do that for them."

"I wish Dad were here, don't you?"

"No," I said shortly. "If he doesn't want to be here, I don't want him here. I've quit missing him, anyway." That wasn't quite true, but I thought I'd better say it, so Josh wouldn't keep expecting Dad to show up. A couple of times he'd said that he knew Dad wouldn't miss the whole vacation, that he would be here sometime. I knew better.

We covered the worm can, put it on the old table where we clean fish, and started back up the hill. Josh slipped his warm hand into mine. He's kind of a baby sometimes. But it was nice, in a way.

When we got back into the cottage, Mom sent Josh to bed right away. "Last hand, girls," she said. "I'm going to win, anyway."

"Want to play when Mom's done, Kyle?" Vicki asked.

"Sure," I said.

I picked up the score pad. "Jeez, Vicki," I complained. "Sure you can't write any smaller? I can hardly read these numbers."

"At least I don't waste paper that way," she said as she dealt. She had a point. We could probably save a forest a year if everyone wrote as small as she does.

Mom was right—she won on the next hand. She pushed back her chair, kissed us good night, and went into the main room. "Don't stay up too late," she warned as she closed the door behind her.

"I'm tired of five hundred," Andrea said. "How about Yahtzee instead?"

Vicki stopped shuffling. "Okay with me," she said. "Kyle?"

"Yahtzee's good."

So we put away the cards and got out the dice. Yahtzee's a good game for three. You can play and talk at the same time, so you don't get bored when it's not your turn.

"So what really happened with Mrs. Thompson and the toad, Kyle?" Andrea asked as Vicki was rolling.

So I told them, and when I got to the point where Mrs. Thompson was up on the chair, screaming, "Get him! Get him!" I climbed up on my chair to imitate her and we all laughed so loud that Mom called, "Quiet in there!"

We settled down and played a couple of games, but I got sleepy pretty quick. When you're getting up to fish around five every morning, you don't feel like staying up late. At the end of the third game, which I won, I shoved the dice over to Vicki and said, "Enough for me. I'm going to bed."

Vicki and Andrea exchanged a glance. It almost felt like

they were relieved I was leaving. It made me feel a little peculiar. Andrea was my twin, not Vicki's. "You two going to stay up?" I asked in what I hoped was a casual tone.

"For a while," Vicki said.

"Are you going out fishing early, Kyle?" Andrea asked.

"You want to go along?"

"No, but wake me up when you leave, will you?"

"Wake you? Why?"

"Ask me no questions; I'll tell you no lies," she said in a teasing voice. As soon as she said it, I realized. My birthday was less than a month away. She was planning something. Of course, if it were my real birthday, it would be Andrea's, too, but when we were just little, Mom had suggested we pick separate birthdays, anytime in the year, so that we would each have a day that was ours alone. I was glad she'd done it, because our real birthday was the day after Christmas, and who wants a birthday then? I'd picked July 19, because nineteen is my lucky number, and that way we could celebrate at the lake. Andrea'd picked September 19, so she could be like me but have a school birthday. That's important when you're little.

What could she be planning? It's not like we had lots of places to shop around here. Oh, well, knowing Andrea, it would be something I'd like. She always knew. Too bad she didn't have the money to pay the taxes on the cottage. That's what I really wanted.

I guess not every family makes a big deal out of birthdays, but ours does. Last January we'd had a really big celebration for Dad's fortieth birthday. It was a surprise party, and all the neighbors came and brought silly getting-old gifts like a magnifying glass, in case his sight got bad, and a box of prunes, in case he began to have trouble that way. (I'm not sure Dad thought that one was funny, but everyone else did.)

I started thinking. January 10. Thirty-five days later he left. That night, when he was blowing out candles and laughing and joking, was he already planning to leave us? I thought back. Vicki and Andrea and I had helped pour sodas and pass around snacks. I thought Dad was having a good time—he actually ate a piece of the cake Mom made for him, although he hardly ever eats sweets. He doesn't even put sugar on his cereal. Anyway, that night he did have a piece of the cake, and he told jokes and laughed and thanked everyone for coming. After the party we helped Mom clean up. When the kitchen was finished, we said good night, and Mom said she was tired, too. "I'm going on to bed now," she called into the living room. "Coming, hon'?"

"In a while," he said. He was sitting in the big red chair,

and he'd taken off his shoes and picked up the evening paper.

But it was later than "a while," I guess, because around two, when I got up to go to the bathroom (I'd had three Cokes), the living room light was still on, and I could hear Mom and Dad talking.

Mom was saying, "I worry when you're like this. Remember what they say: Life begins at forty."

And Dad said, "So does middle age."

She took a long time to answer, but then she asked quietly, "Is that so bad?"

Just then I realized I was sort of eavesdropping, and besides, my feet were getting cold, so I went on into the bathroom and shut the door. I wish now I'd listened longer.

I was remembering all this when I heard giggling in the kitchen. Whatever Vicki and Andrea were planning for my birthday (if that's what they were doing), it must be something funny.

I yawned. It had been a long day. The kitchen light shone through the window above me, so I turned my head away and pulled the covers up. The light stayed on for a long time, and I fell asleep to the sound of whispering.

CHAPTER SEVEN

THE NEXT MORNING I HEADED to Clyde's with my night crawlers in one can and a mess of red worms in another. I'd dug the worms up between fishing and breakfast. Mom hadn't been too happy about having her mixing bowl filled with ground coffee. She'd opened one of the doors in the lower section of the cabinet and pointed to five or six empty cans stored there. Well, how was I supposed to know?

How much money would I get for the worms? I wondered now. It wouldn't be much, but it would be something. In the back of my mind a bright red dollar sign with *400* after it flashed like a neon sign. That was a lot of night crawlers.

I was so busy thinking, I was at Clyde's before I knew it. And I was hot and thirsty. Still, I wouldn't waste money on a Coke. I'd sell my bait and get out of there. Clyde was sitting on a stool behind the counter, the newspaper spread out in front of him. "Damn politicians," he said by way of greeting. "They're ruining the country. What can I do for you today, Kyle?"

"I brought some worms," I said. "Thirty night crawlers and fifty red worms." I put my cans on the counter. "Do you want to count them?"

Clyde laughed. "I wouldn't insult Hazel Cook's grandson by counting. Your word is good enough for me." He opened up the cash register and took out some bills and change. "Here you go," he said. "A dollar fifty a dozen for night crawlers makes three seventy-five, and fifty red worms at four cents apiece comes to two dollars." He put the money in my outstretched hand, then pivoted around on the stool so he could reach the refrigerator. He pulled out a root beer and handed it to me. "And a bonus for promptness," he said, chuckling.

"Thanks, Mr. Stemm, thanks a lot," I said. "I'll bring you some more tomorrow."

"When you can," he said with a sideways wave of his brown-freckled hand. "I'll be here."

I turned to leave. "Oh, by the way," he said. "Tom Butler said if you came in, he wanted you to stop by his cottage on the way home. Said he had a proposition that might interest you."

"Okay," I said doubtfully, wondering what kind of

proposition he could have in mind. We'd never had much to do with Mr. Butler. Not that he wasn't all right—he just kept to himself, that's all. And, speaking frankly, I'd always thought he was kind of gross, since he was so fat. Still, I'd see what he wanted.

* * *

Tom Butler's cottage was one of those that had been converted into a year-round home. He'd done that after his wife died—said he'd only kept the house in Elkhart to please her. For himself, the lake was enough. I remembered Mrs. Butler pretty well. She'd been a little woman, with black hair drawn back into a bun. She always wore red, and she had a way of laughing that made you want to laugh along with her. She made good chocolate-chip cookies, too. She'd only been dead a couple of years. Walking up the gravel driveway to the cottage, I admired how neat and trim it was. Mrs. Butler had always grown flowers next to the cottage, and Tom Butler kept up her flower garden real pretty. I knocked at the screen door to the kitchen. I could smell bacon, and my mouth watered.

"C'mon in. It's open," Mr. Butler called.

I stepped into a kitchen so big it was a wonder the cottage had space for any other rooms. There was a fancy stove over in the corner and a mammoth refrigerator and

60

lots and lots of cupboards. Mr. Butler was sitting at the table. He had on a sleeveless undershirt, and springy gray chest hairs curled up around the top. His arms were as big around as loaves of bread. He hadn't shaved that day, and a dribble of egg yolk stained the whiskers on his chin. He gestured at a pile of toast sitting on a plate in the center of the table. "Morning, Kyle. Sit down and have a piece of toast. That honey's special from Missouri. Try it."

I did as I was told. We chewed companionably for a while, and then he said, "Clyde told you I wanted to see you, hmm?"

"Yes, sir."

You could tell he wasn't used to talking a lot. It was like he didn't know how to begin. "Thing is, I promised my daughter. That I wouldn't go out on the lake alone anymore. Since I had that dizzy spell."

He seemed to feel he had said enough, but I was puzzled.

"You want me to go fishing with you?"

"Yep."

"When?"

"Every day. Can't stand living by the lake and not being out on it. You know how to be quiet, don't you?"

"I think so."

"Don't want someone blathering to me all the time. I see

you leaving early. That's when I like to go. Dawn till breakfast. About five hours. Pay you five dollars a day."

I just stared at him. Five dollars a day? How many days would we be here? The neon numbers began flashing down—*395, 390, 385* . . . "Great," I managed to say. "When do you want to start?"

"Tomorrow."

"I'll be here."

"One thing. You'll have to row. I don't like motors."

I had to hide disappointment. We had a motor for our boat, but I wasn't allowed to use it. Mom hadn't even had anyone put it on this summer. For a minute there, I'd pictured me and him cruising down to the far end of the lake. If we were just going to row, we'd have to stick fairly close by. Oh, well—I'd be doing what I loved to do and getting paid for it. How lucky could I get?

"Thanks a lot, Mr. Butler," I said.

"Call me Tom."

I let myself out of the kitchen and loped back up the road. I could hardly wait to tell Mom. She was down by the lake, sitting in the shade of the hickory, reading a book. "Hey, Mom!" I called, hurrying down the steps. "Guess what? I've got a job!"

"A job?" She put down her book and took off her sunglasses to look at me. "What kind of a job?" I told her all about it, beginning with what Clyde said. "Are you sure you won't mind being tied down that way? I thought your mornings alone on the lake were pretty special to you."

"Being with Mr. Butler will almost be like being alone," I said. "He hardly talks, and he doesn't want me to talk much either."

She laughed. "That sounds like him."

"Tell me about him," I asked.

"You know a lot already."

"Tell me what he was like when you were little and knew him."

"Well, let me see—he was never very talkative, not even when his wife was alive. Her name was Mary Ann, and their daughter, Lou, is just a bit older than I. They had a float out on the lake then, and Lou and I used to swim together sometimes. When we'd finished swimming, we'd sunbathe on their pier, and Mary Ann would bring us down some of her cookies and tall glasses of cold milk. Then she'd stay and talk—she loved to talk, and I don't suppose she got much conversation out of Tom. I always wondered if he was so quiet before the war, when they got married."

"Before the war?"

"The Second World War, honey. Tom Butler was in the

Air Force. I think he was shot down over Germany. I know he was a prisoner of war for a long time. He never talked about it, though. At least not to me. I don't think even Lou knows much."

I was quiet. It was strange to think that someone I knew was old enough to have been in World War II. How old was he?

I asked Mom. "Oh, he's probably in his fifties or sixties now, I suppose. I think he was older than most when he enlisted. What kind of dizzy spell did he have, did he say?"

"Nope."

"Well, I guess you'll be all right. He'll be sitting all the time you're in the boat. But you make sure you both wear life preservers, you hear?" I had to grin. The only time Mom says "you hear?" is when we're up at the lake. Gram used to say that, too.

"Hey, Kyle, put on your suit and come in with us!" Andrea yelled from down the shore a bit, where she and Vicki and Josh were swimming. Or where she and Vicki were swimming, and Josh was paddling. I remembered about wanting to help him with his swimming this summer.

"Down in a minute," I called. I gave Mom a quick kiss on the top of the head and started up to the cottage. Thinking about the money I'd be earning, I began to whistle. It looked like maybe we could save the cottage after all. Just like I'd thought.

* * *

A little later I was standing in the lake. Josh was standing in front of me, his arms folded stubbornly across his chest. "You have to put your face in the water," I told him for the hundredth time. He'd just showed me how far he could already "swim." "If you try to hold your neck up like that all the time, you'll get tired. You want to be able to swim a long way and a long time."

"Like Dad did?"

"Yeah."

"Did he really swim all the way across the lake?"

"Yep. Mom rowed the boat alongside him in case he needed to stop, but he didn't."

Josh turned his head to look out across the lake. His eyes narrowed. "Did he swim fast so no fish could bite him?"

"Fish in this lake don't bite people."

"Sharks bite."

"But there aren't any sharks."

"There might be, and you just don't know."

"Sharks live in salt water. We have bass and bluegills and perch and pike and catfish—like that."

"And turtles."

"Yeah, and turtles."

"Turtles bite. A snapping turtle could bite off your toes."

I had an inspiration. "That's why you need to put your face in the water—so you can see what's around you."

He thought about that, then said, "Okay," kind of doubtfully. He uncrossed his arms, bent his neck, then stopped. "Kyle?"

"What now?"

"What if I swallow some water?"

"You swallow water every day."

"But this water might have stuff in it."

"Like what?"

"Fish poop."

I worked hard to keep my face straight. I didn't want him to see me laugh. "Fish don't poop around here," I told him. "They go out to the middle to do that."

Okay, so I was making that up, but I didn't know what else to say, and it seemed to satisfy him. He ducked his head down, and after a bit he got the hang of duck-breathe-duck. But later the sun disappeared, and when he stood I could see goose bumps on his shoulders, and his lips were blue. "Time to get out," I said. "Race you to shore."

I didn't let him win, of course, but I let him come close. That's what Dad used to do with me.

CHAPTER EIGHT

WHEN I AWOKE IT TOOK ME a minute or so to figure out what I was hearing. Then I realized. It was the *plip-plop* of raindrops falling on the wooden shutters outside the screens. Crud! Mr. Butler probably wouldn't want to go out in the rain. What time was it? I didn't hear any birds, and it wasn't quite light out. I'd set our little alarm clock just in case, though I'd been pretty sure I wouldn't need it. It hadn't gone off yet. Couldn't be too late. I rolled over to look. Quarter till five. I thought of going back to sleep. It was nice and warm under the covers. But I was wide awake. I decided to go ahead and get up. I'd go down to Mr. Butler's, see if he was out, and if he wasn't, I'd take our rowboat and go by myself. It didn't sound like much of a rain.

A little later, crunching my way up Mr. Butler's gravel driveway, I was glad I'd gotten up. He stepped out the door like he'd been waiting. Like me, he had a raincoat on. At home I wouldn't be caught dead in a raincoat, but up here I liked wearing Gram's old yellow one. She'd called it her slicker. It was made out of some heavy, shiny material, and it had a hat that stuck out over your eyes to keep the rain out of your face, with a long flap on back to keep your neck dry.

"Morning," I said.

He grunted and handed me his tackle box. I carried the box and my pole in my right hand and a can of worms in my left. We made our way down the hill in silence. At the bottom of the hill, he motioned for me to go on out to the boat. He had eight or ten cane poles standing up against a small shed, and he kind of looked them over before he picked out one and brought it to the boat, which I'd already untied from the pier.

I held up my hand to steady him as he stepped down in, but he ignored it. The boat rocked only a little; he had good balance. He settled himself in the stern and I poled us out to deeper water, then put the oars into the oarlocks and began rowing. It was a lot harder with him in the boat, let me tell you. When I was out from between piers, I asked him, "Where to?"

"Let's anchor off shore down by Johnson's Point. I hear the bluegills are biting."

The shore was a dim outline on my left as I pulled steadily at the oars. The mist was heavy this morning, and the raindrops made little bull's-eyes in the water. A few other boats were setting out, too, most of them outboards, of course. Hooded figures waved as they emerged from the mist and then passed on into it again, the motors dwindling into the distance. In the stern, Mr. Butler sat still, his legs spread wide to accommodate his overhanging stomach, his hands on his thighs.

"Right about here," he said in a bit, and I shipped the oars and we let down the anchors. We were maybe twenty-five feet out from the reeds. There was a drop-off on our right, I knew, and I wondered whether he planned to fish shallow in by the reeds or deeper on the other side. I didn't wait to see what he would do. I'd already made up my mind to fish just in from the reeds. But shortly after my bobber hit the water, his splashed down only a little ways off. It felt good to see that his choice was the same as mine.

I don't want to brag, but I'm a pretty good fisherman. I learned from Gram. From Dad, too, but Gram was the best. I guess once when I was little, I told a friend that everyone had to do what Gram said because she was the Boss of the Lake. Since she really could be kind of bossy, that became a family joke.

"I know this lake like I know my own backyard," she'd say. "Been fishing it for sixty years." Dad had taught me how to bait my hook and set my bobber and handle my pole, but Gram had taught me about fish. She taught me that perch like to hide in the underwater grasses near shore, that bass go deeper as the morning passes, that the bigger the bluegill, the more boldly he takes the bait, and that when you're fishing shallow you don't yank at every little dip of your bobber—you wait for a rapid downward plunge.

We anchored there by the reeds for an hour or so, while the rain fell gently and the sky lightened. Then at about six, when the sun was just rising over the far end of the lake and a mother duck led a line of ducklings into the water down near the lily pads, the fish began to bite. I caught the first, a good-size sunfish, and then Mr. Butler caught two bluegills. I was freshening my bait when I saw his bobber suddenly disappear. Whatever had his bait, it wasn't fooling around. He didn't act excited at all, just stretched one leg out to brace himself and began pulling. I watched, intent. The line wasn't circling, it went straight out from the boat. His pole was bent.

"What do you think it is?" I asked.

"Turtle," he said, disgusted. "And a big one. I'll be lucky if he doesn't break my line." Sure enough, in a few minutes

I saw the broad greenish back of the turtle, just as the line snapped and Tom's pole sprang upward.

"Waste of good bait," he grumbled. "I woulda liked to get the hook out of him."

The rain stopped about then, and the sun turned the horizon all pinkish gold. I love the way morning happens. One minute everything around you is gray—sky, water, shoreline, trees. Next thing you know, like magic, all the color is back—deep blue water, green and brown cattails, orange life jackets in a heap on a white pier, and you didn't see it happen. Too bad Andrea wasn't here. I'll bet if she had been, she could have shown me. She'd have said, "Look, Kyle. Morning's happening," and I'd look up just in time to see it, see everything change.

The fish stopped biting. We pulled up anchor and I rowed us over to the west side of the island, where it drops off pretty steep, and we caught a couple perch there. We'd taken off our raincoats by then, and the sun was beginning to feel hot on my neck. Mr. Butler's stomach grumbled. I could hear it clear down at the other end of the boat. "Time for breakfast," he said, and pulled in his line.

I stared at him. Breakfast? He'd been eating ever since we came out. From one raincoat pocket, he'd pulled a thermos of coffee; from the other, a couple of bologna sandwiches

71

and a bag of cookies. He'd offered me a cookie, but I'd shaken my head, and he hadn't offered again. He'd eaten the whole bag, and I mean a whole bag like you buy at the grocery. There must've been two dozen cookies in there. He'd finished his thermos of coffee, too.

Dad and I never ate in the boat. We'd fish till we were famished—lake air will do that to you—then we'd go in, clean a couple perch or some bluegills, and take them up to the cottage. If we hadn't caught anything that morning, we could get something out of the live-box. Between the two of us, we kept it full. Dad would fry the fish in cornmeal till they were brown and crispy on the outside, white and flaky inside. They were the best! We'd eat until we were full, then push back our plates and just sit and talk until the others woke up. Well, I was famished again today, but I didn't see how Tom could be. And he sure wasn't going to sit and talk to anyone.

I wrapped the line around my pole, pulled up anchor, and began to row toward home. About halfway across the lake, he said, "Glad to see you use a pole. Any fool can catch a fish with a rod and reel."

It was the last thing he said to me that morning. We finished the ride in silence, and when we got to shore, he climbed out without a word and left me to tie the boat up as he mounted the hill to his cottage.

I went home happy, knowing I was five dollars richer. He'd said he would pay me by the week, and that was okay with me. I carried my pole and my bait can and my raincoat, and I just kind of jogged along, I felt so good. I had no way of knowing what had happened at the cottage while I was gone.

CHAPTER NINE

NO ONE WAS INSIDE WHEN I got back. The breakfast dishes had been done and were drying in the dish rack. I went through the main room to the porch and looked down toward the lake. Vicki was sitting in the shade, reading (big surprise), and Andrea's head was bent over her sketchbook. Josh was climbing around on the hill, probably looking for another toad, but I didn't see Mom at all.

I decided to get something to eat, then go down and see if Josh wanted me to take him out for a boat ride. I might even let him try to row a little. I planned to make another trip to the island this afternoon. I'd wear swim trunks, anchor the boat up close, and wade around it as far as I could. I knew that on our side of the island the bottom was stony and the water was shallow, but I wasn't sure about the far side. Whistling a little tune (I've got a pretty good whistle, and I like to keep in practice), I got out the bread and the peanut butter jar. Peanut butter toast is one of my all-time favorite snacks. I made two pieces, and after I ate the first, I decided I'd probably want more. I'd just stuck two new slices under the broiler when Mom came in the kitchen door.

"Where were you? I didn't see you down by the lake," I said.

"I was over at the Morleys', taking a telephone call."

"Oh," I said, chewing. "Who called?"

"Don't talk with your mouth full, Kyle. It was Dave Becker."

"The Realtor? He's not going to bring someone else to see the cottage, is he?"

"No, he doesn't have anyone else who wants to see it." She had her back to me when she said that, getting a cup out of the cupboard.

"That's good." I pulled the broiler drawer wider and flipped the toast. When I looked again, Mom was still facing the cupboard, the cup in her hand.

I had a funny feeling. Had her voice sounded strange? "Mom? If he didn't have anyone who wants to come see the cottage, why'd he call?"

"The Thompsons have made an offer on the cottage, Kyle. They want to buy it."

"Wha—No!" I sputtered. "They wouldn't! They didn't like it at all. I heard them say so."

"They don't like it," she said. "They want to buy it for the lot. Then they'll tear it down and build something else."

"Tear it down? No!" My stomach felt as if I were going to be sick. "They can't do that, can they?"

"If they buy it and have the money, they can."

"But you won't let them, will you, Mom? That would be awful."

"I don't know, Kyle. I'll have to think. Dave Becker says he doubts we'll get anyone else willing to pay the asking price. People expect cottages to be a little more up-to-date these days."

"You can't think about it, Mom. Just tell them no. I'll never forgive you if you let them do it, never! It would be bad enough if someone bought it to live in, but to tear it down . . . Besides—"

"Besides what? Get your toast, honey—it's burning."

I pulled out blackened slices of bread that scorched my fingertips before I could drop them on the plate. After I'd turned off the broiler, I finished my thought. "Besides, maybe we won't have to sell. Maybe something will happen."

Out on the lake this morning, I'd come up with a plan. I was pretty sure that between Tom Butler and my worm sales, I could raise two hundred dollars this summer. And once we got back home, Vicki and Andrea could probably earn something too—babysitting, or whatever. I was counting on them for one hundred each. That would take care of the fall bill. We'd deal with spring later. I wanted to tell Mom now, but I hadn't talked to Vicki or Andrea yet. What if they couldn't save that much? What if they didn't want to? I should have talked to them before. I had kind of relaxed when I found out the Thompsons didn't like the cottage, and no one else had come around looking.

Now I felt myself getting desperate. "Please, Mom? Say you won't let them tear it down."

I gave her my most pleading look, but she looked away. "I have to think, Kyle," she repeated stubbornly.

I can be stubborn, too. "Remember what I said about not forgiving you. Think about that. Think hard," I said. "I'm going down to the lake."

Ordinarily I wouldn't talk to Mom like that. Ordinarily she wouldn't let me. But she was upset, and she must have known I was, too, because she just pressed her lips tight and let me go.

Down at the lake, things went wrong at first. Andrea hadn't heard me coming, but when my shadow fell over her sketchbook, she looked up and slammed the book shut.

"You shouldn't sneak up on people like that!" she said.

"I wasn't sneaking up. You were just wrapped up in what you were drawing. What was it anyway?"

"Nothing," she said, pushing her hair away from her face.

What was bugging her? I never looked in her sketchbook unless she wanted me to. She sat hugging it to her chest like she thought I'd take it out of her arms. "Well, then, be like that," I said. "Who wants to see your old drawings anyway? We have more important things to think about."

She didn't answer, just sat there glaring at me.

"Vicki?" I said. "Hey, Vicki, put your book down and listen to me."

"Can't a person have a little time to herself around here? I want to finish this before lunch."

"Finish later," I told her. "This is important."

"Oh, all right. What's up? How was the fishing?"

"The fishing was fine, but everything else is lousy. Mom got an offer on the cottage."

"She did? From the people who came yesterday?" Now Andrea looked concerned. "Is she going to take it?"

"I don't know."

"But you said they didn't like the cottage."

"They don't. They want to tear it down and build a new one on the lot."

They stared at me. Andrea's face got so pale her freckles looked like wet sand sprinkled over her cheeks and nose. "Tear it down?" she whispered.

Vicki closed her book without bothering to mark her place. "We need a way to stop them. There's got to be something we can do," she fumed.

"There is," I said eagerly. "I've been thinking."

"I knew you'd have an idea!" Andrea exclaimed.

As I outlined my plan, I could tell they weren't exactly enthusiastic. I tried to be persuasive. I talked about the good times we'd always had here. I pointed out that Josh was just getting to the age when he could really enjoy it. Andrea twirled a lock of hair around her finger, the way she does when she's thinking. Vicki looked out at the lake without any expression at all. I almost wondered if she was even listening to me.

"A hundred dollars is a lot of money," Andrea said finally. "How soon would I have to have it?"

Good old Andrea. I knew I could count on her. "Sometime in the fall," I said. "Could you get it by then?"

"I don't know," she said doubtfully. "I can't earn much babysitting after school, and even if I persuade Mom to let me sit in the evenings, too, Vicki will get most of the jobs. But I do have some money in my savings account."

"That's for college!" Vicki told her. "Mom would never let you spend that!"

"Well, if you don't think we can do it . . ." I heard my voice trail off. I was getting depressed. What had made me think we could raise four hundred dollars?

"Wait a minute, Kyle," Vicki said. "If Andrea can't save a whole hundred, maybe I could save the rest of her share as well as mine."

"Would you really, Vick? I was afraid . . . I mean, I know you didn't want to come this summer."

"That's different from not being able to come when I do want to. Maybe next year I'll really want to come back."

"Brad and Jeff Marshall just arrived," Andrea told me with a wink. The Marshalls lived a few cottages down. "Their braces are off, and they both grew a foot over the winter."

"That has nothing to do with it!" said Vicki hotly. "I just think the cottage should stay in the family, that's all."

We were all quiet for a moment. I turned around and looked up at the hill. Josh was squatted halfway up, poking in the dirt with a stick. Mom had come out on the front step and was smoking a cigarette. Her head was bent, and she looked discouraged.

I thought of Dad and felt a flash of fury. This was all his fault. He should be here with us, taking care of things.

That's what fathers were supposed to do. They weren't supposed to get all upset and go off by themselves to "think."
So he turned forty. So another publisher turned down his
novel. So what?

I'd written him a letter as soon as I knew the address of
his crummy apartment. I told him instead of writing novels
no one wanted, he should write down the Isabel and Ike
stories he'd been telling us for years. Those stories were so
funny—I loved Ike—I bet any publisher would buy them.
And I told him forty wasn't so old—one of my friends even
had a mother who was fifty! But you know what? He never
even wrote me back—he just told Mom to tell me he ap-
preciated my thoughts. That's when I quit talking to him.

Mom had tried to explain that Dad's life hadn't gone
the way they'd planned it when they first started out. He'd
always wanted to be a writer, and for a couple years he had
stayed home writing while Mom taught. But nothing he
wrote seemed to sell, and then Vicki came along, and then
the rest of us, and he'd had to start teaching, too. He still
tried to find time to write, she said, but it wasn't easy with
a family. He always had papers to grade, and the house and
yard needed attention. Not to mention us, I thought. Well,
if he didn't have time for us, he shouldn't have had us.

Dang! I was doing it again. There was no point in

thinking about Dad, I reminded myself. Dad was history. We'd manage without him. He could sit in his apartment and write all the books he wanted to. I'd never read them.

Vicki got to her feet. "Come on, Andrea. You and I need to talk to Mom. If we tell her Kyle's not the only one who doesn't want to sell to the Thompsons, she'll have to listen."

"How about the taxes?" Andrea asked. "Are we going to tell her we'll pay them?"

"I don't think so," Vicki decided. "Not until we're sure we can earn enough money. Besides, after we pay them in the fall, we'll have to pay them again in the spring, and you won't be fishing with Mr. Butler in the winter, Kyle."

"I'll do something else," I said quickly. "I can earn another two hundred, I know I can."

"Maybe so, but in the meantime, we have to talk Mom out of selling to the Thompsons." That was so like Vicki— most of the time she was off in her own world, and then she'd come charging into yours with her I'm-your-big-sister, let-me-tell-you-what-to-do attitude. This time I didn't mind, though. We needed all the help we could get.

CHAPTER TEN

I TAGGED ALONG WHEN VICKI and Andrea went up to talk to Mom, but they had even less luck than I'd had. They'd hardly begun to talk when Mom got up from her chair and put her hands on her hips. "I told Kyle, and now I'm telling you. I have to think. I know you don't want the cottage torn down. I don't either. But I have the responsibility of keeping this family afloat financially. You've let me know how you feel—now leave me alone for a while."

There are times when you can argue with Mom, and there are times you can't. This was one of the second kind. Andrea bit her lip, Vicki shrugged, and I headed for the door and held it open for them. There was no point in talking anymore, so Vicki went back to her book, and Andrea said she thought she'd go hunt wildflowers to replace the wilted ones in the kitchen. I just sat down on the porch step.

When Josh saw me there, he scrambled up the hill and sat beside me. "Want to kick the soccer ball?" he asked. "Like yesterday?"

What I wanted to do was sulk in silence, but Josh looked so hopeful I hated to spoil his day as well as my own. "Let's get the boat and give you a rowing lesson instead," I answered.

Instantly he was speeding down the steps. "Wait a minute," I called. "Why don't you put on your trunks? Maybe we can do a little swimming, too."

He stopped in his tracks, turned, and sped up the steps. You sure could tell he wanted to go. After we'd changed, I called into the kitchen, "Hey, Mom, I'm taking Josh rowing."

"Wear your life jackets!" she called back.

When I got to the bottom of the hill, Josh was already in the boat, sitting smack in the middle of the center seat. I lifted an eyebrow. (I'd practiced a long time to learn how to do that.) "You already know what to do?" I asked.

"Well, sort of."

"Go ahead, then." I climbed in and sat down in the stern.

Josh put a hand on an oar. "You have to untie us first," I reminded him.

"Oh, yeah." Josh blushes easy. He used the rope to pull us over to the pier, undid the knot, and pushed us away.

Then he pulled an oar out of the oarlock and started poling. The oar was big for him, and he stuck out his tongue in concentration, but he shoved us into open water pretty well. Then he sat back down and started to row.

It was obvious pretty quickly that Josh's right arm was stronger than his left. The boat was beginning to circle, so I showed him how you find a point and fix on it. That's the only hard part of rowing, keeping the boat going straight. Well, I guess if you're seven, rowing itself is hard. I'd forgotten. I'll say this for Josh, he's not a quitter. I let him follow the shoreline for fifteen minutes or so, then we switched.

"Will you row us over to the island? Please?" Josh begged.

"Sure, if you want."

On the ride over Josh sat perfectly still, staring ahead at the island. Something about his bulky orange life jacket made him look skinnier than ever, and I reminded myself not to let him stay in the water so long that he got cold. I love lake weather, but it never gets hot here the way it does in Florida. Michigan always has a little chill in reserve, ready to throw at you.

When we were close enough that the water was only a couple of feet deep, I asked, "Want to get out?" Josh didn't bother to answer, just jumped over the side. I anchored the boat and got out, too.

The lake bottom around the island is rough and stony. It doesn't make for comfortable wading, but on the south side it slopes down so gradually that it's a good place to practice swimming. That's what I had in mind for Josh next. First, though, we waded around a bit. Trees and brambly undergrowth crowded together, reaching right to the water's edge in a sort of inhospitable way. It was like the island was saying "Keep off," and it was easy to believe that no one had ever set foot on it. Or had someone? I waded close to the spot where I used to think I could see a path. If there had been one, it was overgrown now. Still, it looked like the most likely spot to begin, whenever I had a chance to explore. I didn't let Josh in on my plan. When I stepped onto the island for the first time, I was going to be alone.

I was planning what I'd need to bring with me when cold water splashed on my back. I turned. Josh had pulled the bailing can from the boat and was filling it with more water to throw at me. He had the biggest smile I'd seen on his face for a long time. "I'll show you!" I called and went after him. We splashed and chased until he'd had enough and yelled "Uncle!" Then I told him we were going to have another swimming lesson.

"I don't need more lessons. I know how to swim now."

"But you need to know more than one stroke. If you

know the side stroke, you can use it as a kind of resting stroke on a long swim," I answered.

I can't say he improved any, but at least he tried. After about half an hour, I decided he'd had enough, and I let him wade around and pull up stones. He said he wanted to take one home as a souvenir, but it had to be a special one. He couldn't explain what a "special" one would look like, but he seemed to have no doubt he'd find one. He was still looking when I heard the bell from the cottage. A long time ago Gram had bought a big old bell at a country auction, and she'd had Grandpa mount it on a post down by the pier so she could call him in from the lake when she needed him. Mom said he had grumbled about it but finally admitted it was useful, and from then on he and everyone else had called it "Hazel's telephone."

"Must be lunchtime," I said. "Mom's ringing for us."

Back in the boat I expected Josh to want to row again, but he must have been tired, because he plopped down in the stern without a word. We were about halfway back when he asked me, "Kyle, what were you and Vicki and Andrea talking about this morning?"

"Those people who looked at the cottage," I said. "They want to buy it so they can tear it down and build a new one on the lot."

"Why do they want to do that? It's a good cottage."

"They don't think so."

"Well, we can all just sit down in the middle and not move, and then they can't tear it down."

"I wish it were as easy as that," I answered, careful not to grin.

"You won't let them do it, will you, Kyle?"

"Not if I can help it."

"What can I do so they won't tear it down?"

I looked at him. His jaw was set the way it is when he's dribbling the ball down the soccer field. It made him look older, somehow. I thought about what he asked. "I know what you can do," I said. "We're all trying to earn money so Mom won't have to sell. You can catch crickets."

"Crickets?" He looked a little uncertain.

"Sure, I'll show you how to do it. You can use Gram's old cricket cage, and after you've caught a bunch, I'll sell them to Clyde Stemm for you."

"I want to sell them myself. They're my crickets."

"Not until you catch them, they aren't." This time I did grin at him.

When we reached the pier, I tried to show him how I tie the boat up with a half hitch at each end. But he'd listened to me enough for one day. His mind was on crickets.

Up at the cottage Mom had tuna salad sandwiches and tomato soup ready. As soon as Andrea saw me come into the kitchen, she shook her head at me, moving her eyes in Mom's direction. She was telling me not to ask anything. It was a quiet meal. Even Josh seemed solemn. Finally Mom shook her head, like she was coming out of a daydream. "How was the rowing lesson?" she asked.

"Me and Kyle had a great time, didn't we?" Josh said.

"Kyle and I," Mom said automatically. Whenever we make a grammar mistake, she always repeats what we said the correct way, and then we say it right after her. Her heart didn't really seem in it today, but Josh went ahead and corrected himself.

"Kyle and I," he said. "I'm getting real good, aren't I, Kyle?"

"Pretty good," I answered.

"Andrea and I are going to swim out to Marshalls' float and hang around there for a while this afternoon," Vicki said. "Want to come along, Kyle?"

She didn't sound too enthusiastic about having me join them. "Nope," I answered. "Even if Jeff and Brad have their braces off, they're a couple of snobs as far as I'm concerned."

"They are not!"

"I said, as far as I'm concerned. You don't have to think

so if you don't want. But I know them better than you." A couple of summers ago I'd hung out with those guys, till I finally figured out that if they couldn't brag about all the things their family owns, they wouldn't have any conversation at all. Vicki would just have to learn that for herself.

Mom had sort of dropped out of the conversation again. Maybe she really was thinking hard. "I'm going to lie down for a while," she said now, pushing back her chair.

It was Andrea's turn to do the dishes, so she started clearing the table.

"Come on, Josh, let's get the cricket cage," I said.

Two hours and twenty-three crickets later, Josh lost interest. I told him to go get some lettuce to put in the cage and to be sure to keep the cage in the shade. Clyde Stemm wouldn't pay for fried crickets.

After the crickets, Josh talked Andrea into playing Crazy Eights. I got out the push mower and did the bit of lawn between the bottom of the hill and the lake edge. Then I lay down on the pier to sun myself a little, and I fell asleep. It's a good thing I don't burn easily like Vicki does, because I slept for quite a while, I guess. Andrea woke me up by scooping up some water and dribbling it on my back.

"Supper's finally ready. It's way late," she said. "But first Mom wants to talk to us."

We climbed the steps together. "Has she decided?" I asked.

"I think so," Andrea said. "But I don't know which way."

Mom was sitting in the rocker on the porch. Andrea and I dropped down on my bed. Vicki took the other rocker, and Josh sat on the floor, leaning back against the bed.

Mom took a deep breath. "I've decided to turn down the offer," she said.

Vicki ran over and hugged Mom. Andrea clapped. I sat up and rumpled Josh's hair. "Hear that?" I asked him. "Mom's not going to let the Thompsons tear the cottage down."

"However," Mom said, rubbing the back of her neck. "The cottage is still for sale. It's my hope that a family will buy it, a family who will love it as much as we have. You kids will have to accept that. This is our last summer here, so enjoy it as much as you can."

I scowled. Why did she have to say that?

"I don't want you to think," she went on, "that this changes anything. I'm still determined to sell. It's just that I couldn't bear to see it torn down."

After that, there wasn't much to say. I didn't know how I felt as we sat down to eat. Sure, the cottage was saved temporarily, but Mom was right. Nothing had really changed.

CHAPTER ELEVEN

NOT MUCH HAPPENED THE NEXT couple weeks as far as the cottage was concerned. Nobody else came to look at it, and I began to hope nobody would. Maybe everyone was like the Thompsons and wanted something fancier, more up-to-date. I'll admit, I wouldn't have minded having running water and a bathroom instead of the outhouse, but those things weren't a big deal to me. Why complain about pumping buckets of water or spending a few minutes in an outhouse if you got fishing and swimming and a view of the lake in exchange?

Once or twice on weekends, a strange car or two would drive down the road and slow down by the "For Sale" sign. Then I'd worry for a couple hours, but when no telephone call came, I'd relax again. My worry didn't go away then, but it kind of subsided, the way a dog will lie down and just growl low in his throat when he decides he can quit barking now. When those cars went by, I'd sometimes consider writing Dad again, but I always decided against it. Andrea and Vicki wrote him, though. So did Mom. Even Josh did. Someone was always asking me if I wanted to add a P.S. Mom drove into Cassopolis every day to send everyone's letters and check for mail at the post office there. But she always came back empty-handed. Big surprise.

In the meantime, I was earning money. Every afternoon I'd take my worms and night crawlers and Josh's crickets down to Clyde's. Mornings with Tom Butler had settled into a routine. I'd go by his cottage around five, and he'd be waiting. By the second week I was staying for breakfast with him when we came in from the lake. "Don't like to eat alone," he said when he suggested it. While he made the food, I'd weed his flower bed or bury his garbage across the road or rake his parking area, whatever he wanted that day. It meant more money, and it was nice of him to feed me, I guess, but I was kind of uncomfortable about it.

It was the way he ate. Not just that he ate a lot (he did), but also he ate as if he was afraid someone would grab his plate away from him. He'd sit down to four eggs, six pieces of toast, half a pound of bacon and a quart of orange juice, and he'd be finished eating most of it before I had time to eat one egg and a piece of toast. Then he'd pour himself a big bowl of cereal and eat a couple of doughnuts. He didn't chew with his mouth open or anything gross like that, but he kind of grunted as he ate, and he chewed so fast you didn't see how he had time to swallow. He never talked, so I don't know why he wanted me there, but after he'd finished everything on the table, he'd go over to the stove, pour himself a cup of coffee, and fill the cup with sugar and cream. I did the dishes (I thought I should, since the food was free), and while I did, he'd sit and read the paper.

When I'd finished I'd hang up the dish towel and say, "So long," or something like that, and he'd just make a little noise in his throat, not even looking up at me.

I liked going out with him, though. For one thing, I was learning a lot more about where the fish hang out. When we got in the boat each morning, I'd ask, "Which way?"

Then he'd make his longest speech of the day—something like, "It's pretty cloudy. Bluegills will be close to the surface. Let's go down by the channel." And no matter where we went, we almost always did well.

I was still thinking about him one morning when I got back to the cottage. Mom was in the kitchen by herself. "You look serious," she said. "Something bothering you?"

"Not bothering me," I said. "Just making me wonder. Was Tom Butler always so fat?"

She kind of tucked her lips in, the way she sometimes does when she's thinking. "Fat? No, not always, I don't think. Why?"

"It's just—well, some people, I guess, they can't help being fat. But he could. You should see the way he eats. Dad would have a fit. It's disgusting."

"Disgusting?"

"How much, I mean. And he's always eating—I mean all the time. Every morning out in the boat he eats dough-nuts or cookies, and then he comes in and has this humon-gous breakfast."

"And you think that's wrong?"

"Well, it's not healthy, is it, to be so fat?"

"No, I guess not. But people do strange things some-times. Maybe he's eating because he misses Mary Ann. People sometimes eat when they're lonely."

"But he was fat before she died," I pointed out.

"That's true," Mom admitted. "Why does his eating bother you so much?"

"Because—" I stopped. How could I explain that Tom acted like he never had enough, he was never *full*. I wouldn't be surprised if he got up and ate in the middle of the night. And when I thought that, suddenly I could almost see him sitting in his pajama bottoms and undershirt, a full plate in front of him, the kitchen all dark except for the lamp shining down on his bald head, his fork moving steadily back and forth, back and forth. I couldn't really see that, of course, but for a minute the image was so clear it was almost real, and so sad I blinked my eyes to chase it away.

I started over. "I just think people should take care of their health," I said, looking at the pack of cigarettes lying beside Mom on the table. "Besides, it's gross, how much he eats. He should have a little self-control."

"Judge not, that ye be not judged," she murmured.

When Mom starts quoting the Bible to you, you might as well give up.

To change the subject, I asked her, "Where are Andrea and Vicki?"

"I think they're taking a walk," she said. "They shouldn't be gone long."

"They might have waited for me. They knew I'd be home soon," I grumbled. "They're always off by themselves these days."

"They're probably just talking girl talk and think you'll be bored," Mom said.

I wasn't buying that. She just didn't want me to be mad.

Well, if Andrea and Vicki wanted to keep to themselves, they could go ahead and do it. I didn't care.

Besides, I had other things to think about. I needed a day off. It was almost July already, and I still hadn't explored the island. What I wanted to do was go out early one morning and stay till I had covered every inch of it. But the only days I didn't go out with Tom Butler were Saturdays and Sundays. Neither one of us liked to fish over the weekend. Too many people opened up their cottages for those two days, and they went tearing around the lake in their big speedboats, pulling water-skiers and being loud and obnoxious. So a Saturday or Sunday wouldn't be a good day to explore the island either. I didn't want anyone else to see me and get the same idea. I thought about asking Mr. Butler if I could skip a day. The only thing is, I didn't know what I'd say if he asked why. "I want to explore the island" sounded stupid, like a little kid's plan. I knew there probably wasn't anything there, but a stubborn voice in my mind kept insisting, "Maybe there is."

Well, I'd think of a way to ask when the time came. Monday, I told myself. Monday I'd ask for a day off. That would be my Island Exploration Day. I could hardly wait.

CHAPTER TWELVE

AS IT TURNED OUT, I DIDN'T have to ask for a day off. Saturday morning at about eleven, I was reading in the rocker on the porch when I heard someone knock on the screen door to the kitchen. "Come on in," Mom called from the main room, where she was working on a jigsaw puzzle. I heard her get up and go to the kitchen.

"Why, Tom," she said, "what a nice surprise. Come in and sit down. Have a cup of coffee?"

"Don't mind if I do," came Tom Butler's deep voice. "How're things, Dorrie?"

"Well, you know . . . " Mom sounded a little embarrassed, I thought.

"Yeah, I know. Sorry you have to sell the place. It'll be strange, not having it in the Cook family any more."

"We'll all miss it," Mom said. "Especially Kyle."

"Fine boy you got there, must be proud of him."

"I am. Did you come to see him? I know he's around here someplace."

"That's okay. Just give him a message. I won't be fishing Monday. Got to run into Elkhart."

"I'll tell him. Now, how about a couple of chocolate-chip cookies to go with that coffee? Andrea and Vicki made them, and they're pretty good."

"My Mary Ann always made good cookies."

"Yes, she did. I remember. What do you hear from Lou?"

"She called last night. Said everything's fine."

I had been listening in silent amazement. I never heard Tom Butler talk that much to anyone. After answering about his daughter, though, he fell silent, and Mom didn't say anything either. I pictured them sitting together at the table, sipping their coffee, eating their cookies, not talking. I wondered if his silence made Mom feel fidgety. I felt that way the first few times I went out with him, but not anymore. It was just Tom's way.

I heard his chair push back, heard his grunt as he rose. "Guess your younger boy will be glad to have Kyle home on Monday, hmm?"

"Oh, yes," Mom said with a laugh. "Josh doesn't know what to do with himself when Kyle's gone."

I was startled. I hadn't thought it made any difference

to Josh. He was usually still in his pajamas when I got back from Tom's.

"Tell Kyle to bring the kid along sometime if he likes. Can't learn fishing too young."

"You don't know what you're asking for," said Mom, laughing again. I nodded in agreement, although they couldn't see me.

I heard the screen door open, and then he was gone. "Imagine that!" Mom said to herself. "Who'd believe he'd ask Josh to go fishing?"

"You wouldn't let him go, would you, Mom?" I called.

"Kyle? Are you on the porch? Why didn't you come in and say hello to Mr. Butler?"

"I thought maybe talking to two people at a time might be too much for him."

"Oh, Kyle. Actually, we had quite a nice conversation."

"I know. I heard."

"Then you heard about Monday? Maybe you and Josh can go fishing Monday morning, just the two of you. He'd love it."

"Not Monday! Please, Mom, I've been wanting a day to myself, a whole day to do anything I want. Monday's my chance."

"If not Monday, then when?"

"Tuesday," I promised. "I'll take him out Tuesday afternoon, after the sun cools down."

"I don't want you to take him too far."

I walked into the main room. Mom had sat back down by her jigsaw. "How far is too far?" I teased her. "You don't make any sense sometimes, you know."

She laughed. "Don't get smart, young man. Mothers don't need to make sense."

The front door banged as Josh came up from the lake. "Vicki and Andrea won't do anything," he complained. "They just want to sit and talk."

"Tell you what," I said. "You can walk down to Clyde's with me if you want. Sell your crickets yourself this time."

Mom gave me her oh-that's-nice smile and Josh beamed. "I'll go get them!" he said. "Don't go without me." He dashed out the back door toward the cricket cage.

As I turned to follow him down the hill, Mom said, "Hold on a minute, Kyle." She walked over to the can where we kept the grocery money and took out a dollar. "Here, get two Cokes, one for you and one for Josh. Save your own money."

"Thanks, Mom," I answered. I wondered how she could

be so understanding about some things and yet not understand how miserable I was going to be if she sold the cottage. Tom understood. I'd heard it in his voice. Would Dad? Probably, I thought. He'd understand, but he probably wouldn't care.

CHAPTER THIRTEEN

I WOKE BEFORE THE SUN DID on Monday morning. Outside the screens the night was still black; inside, the air was stay-in-bed cold. I tried turning over and going back to sleep, but I was too excited. I felt like all the adventure stories I had ever read—*Treasure Island, Robin Hood, The Last of the Mohicans*—were about to come true. Ever since I was a little boy, I'd seen the island's tree-covered banks rising from the water, still and mysterious, and dreamed about the day I'd explore them.

Finally that day was today. I made myself stay in bed until the woodpecker who was my personal alarm clock began his rat-a-tat-tat in one of the trees on the hill and a little gray light outlined the screens. Then I threw off the blankets, shivering while I pulled on my jeans and sweatshirt. Once the sun came up, the day would probably be warm enough for shorts or swimming trunks, but I'd need to be well covered if I was going to push my way through the island's heavy brush.

I tiptoed through the main room. Everyone else was asleep, all of them breathing deeply and peacefully as I went by. In the kitchen I opened the fridge to see what I could take along for lunch. To my surprise, a brown paper bag on the top shelf had my name on it in Andrea's handwriting. I opened it up. Two peanut butter sandwiches, an apple, a Coke, and some cookies! She must have made lunch for me after I'd gone to bed. I owed her one for that.

There was leftover homemade pizza in the fridge, too, and I scarfed down three pieces with a glass of milk. That should hold me until lunchtime. Closing the door quietly, I stepped out into the gray morning. I gave my teeth a quick once-over at the pump and headed around the cottage. At the top of the steps, I just stood for a minute, looking down at the lake. The morning was clear, and the island looked large and black on the surface of the gray water. Behind the cottage somewhere the woodpecker was busy tapping for his breakfast. I took a deep breath. This was it!

Out on the pier, I buckled on my life jacket and stepped into the boat. I used the old towel I'd brought to wipe the condensation off the seats. I untied the boat and shoved off.

A light wind was blowing as I rowed across the lake, but that was okay because the rowing was warming me. The sun was rising off to my left; a crow called now and then; only one other boat was out on the lake with me—the whole morning was as perfect as it could be.

Even though I knew where I was going to pull in, I rowed all the way along the southern shore, as close as I could, just looking things over. Now that I was actually ready to land, I almost didn't want to. The feeling of anticipation was so great I was afraid nothing could equal it. But finally I decided. I rowed a little farther in until I felt the bottom scrape the rocks, then I dropped the anchor over and shipped the oars. I jumped from the bow onto the shore of the island. Two steps and I was surrounded by trees. A few more and I lost sight of the water.

How do you explore when you can't see ahead more than two or three feet? If I hadn't brought my compass along, I might have been afraid of getting lost. It was so quiet! That was the first thing that struck me. If there were birds around, my coming had silenced them. Here in the midst of the trees, the light was dim. I took a reading from the compass. Wondering how long it would take me to cross the island, I decided to head straight north. I pushed my way through the bushes, and as I got farther from the shore, I could feel the upward thrust of the island in the calves of my legs.

I'm not a naturalist. I can't say what all I saw. I only know that the bushes were waist- to head-high and prickly. Some of the little plants on the ground were in bloom, but mostly they were just variously shaped and different shades of green. Here and there I saw mushrooms, or what Dad always called shelf fungi, on the sides of trees. Two or three times I spotted holes in the dirt. Some of them were crayfish holes—I recognized them by the mud crust that made them look like little volcanoes—but some were bigger, and I figured they belonged to either snakes or muskrats.

It was probably more than an hour later when I reached the northern shore. I stood on the bank and wiped the perspiration off my forehead. Out of the trees, the breeze felt cool and refreshing. I was glad to be in the open again, with the lake stretching wide before me, but I felt a faint disappointment. I guessed Dad was right. There was nothing on the island.

Still, I wasn't ready to give up. I pushed along the shore, although every other minute or so my way would be blocked and I'd have to cut inland for a while. Finally I reached what I was pretty sure was the westernmost edge of the island. Okay, I thought, this is the plan. I'll cross the island from west to east; that should take me to lunchtime. When I get to the other side, I'll head back to the boat and plan what to do next while I eat.

I was almost reluctant to leave the shore behind me again. I hadn't expected to feel so weird when the trees closed in. Even though I was sure I was the only living thing there, except for the birds and maybe a small animal or two (which I hadn't seen or heard), I still felt kind of claustrophobic in there, as if the canopy of branches were cutting off my air.

About a half hour later, I decided I was getting good and tired of pushing bushes away, and about the same minute I noticed that the bushes were becoming sparser. It was almost as if the area I was walking in now had been thinned out at some time. The trees were farther apart, too, and occasionally I'd see a stump that looked a lot like its tree had been sawed off instead of having fallen. Those puzzled me. Maybe there was no one on the island now, but I was beginning to think somebody had been once. I pushed on. I was getting excited again, like I had been on the boat this morning. I was almost willing to bet that this area had been cleared. It couldn't have happened naturally.

Suddenly, ahead of me, I saw something dark and solid. What was it? It was too far away to see clearly, but it sure was big. It looked like a wall. I frowned. A wall, here? The closer I got, the surer I was. It really was a wall, but not just a single wall; it was the side of a small log cabin!

I moved faster, and soon I was stepping into a clearing. At its center the cabin stood straight and sturdy. It couldn't have been more than ten feet square, I estimated. I circled it, admiring the work that had gone into it. The door to the cabin faced south, and there was a window on the east side. There was no fireplace, no chimney. Along one wall two stout cane poles hung from brackets set in between logs. When I got to the window, I peered in. A cot stretched along the far wall. I could see a rocking chair in one corner and several large wooden crates stacked against another wall. That was all.

I walked around to the door. It had a hook-and-eye closing on the outside. Would I be trespassing if I went in? I guessed so, but I also guessed it wouldn't matter. Clearly no one had been here in a long time, maybe years. The hook and eye were rusted, and I had some trouble separating them. The door squeaked as I pushed it back. I hesitated on the doorsill. The interior of the cottage was dim and musty-smelling. I'd just take a quick look around, I decided. I thought of Goldilocks and had to smile, but I left the door open wide behind me.

I went over to the cot first. At its foot a heavy blanket lay neatly folded. I touched it, and it felt stiff and scratchy. Still, it would be warm. A thinnish pillow without a pillow case lay at the head of the bed. In a corner of the room stood a broom, an ax, and a spade. Tools, cot, rocker, crates—a man's place, for sure. The wooden crates intrigued me. I went over and looked at them. The tops weren't nailed down, so I lifted one off. The crate was full of cans. I took one out, blew on its lid, read the faded label. Pork and Beans in Tomato Sauce. Another can held fruit cocktail. One after the other, I lifted them out. They were all food of one sort or another. Looked like someone planned to spend quite some time here. I checked the other crates. The first just held more cans of food. The last held a can opener, a tin of matches, some candles, some empty cans, some hooks and bobbers in a cardboard box, and some old paper sacks. Looking at the matches gave me a thought. I replaced everything carefully and went outside. Sure enough, near the eastern side of the cabin, where it would be protected from the wind, a circle of stones marked the place where someone had probably once had a campfire.

I sat down on the ground and leaned my back against the cabin. Who had built it here? And when? It must have been before Dad started coming to the lake. He'd told me over and over again that there was nothing here, and he'd had no reason to lie about it.

Well, whoever built it had wanted to be sure he'd have enough provisions to stay for two or three weeks. Was it a fishing camp? Maybe.

A rumble from my stomach reminded me to take a look at the sky. I was surprised to find that the sun was already inching over to the west. Reluctantly I stood up and went over to the door, hooking it shut again. I started back into the trees in the direction of the boat, my mind full of questions and plans. The most important question was, would Mom let me spend the night here sometime? And if she would, was I brave enough to sleep out here alone, beyond calling distance? Maybe a walkie-talkie, or Gram's bell, if I had something like that . . .

The hike back to the boat felt short—I guess because I was so preoccupied. When I got there, I sat in the boat and ate my lunch. I'd put my Coke in the water earlier, so it was nice and cold. It was a knockout lunch. I made a mental note to thank Andrea.

After lunch I just waded around for a while, getting my jeans all wet, of course. When I got tired of that, I climbed back into the boat and pulled up the anchor. I'd planned to spend the whole day on the island, but now that I'd found the cabin, I was satisfied. I'd go back to the cottage now and maybe take Josh out for a little fishing just beyond the end of the pier.

As I rowed back to shore, the thought of the cabin was like a little sunlit place in my mind. I knew I'd have to tell the others about it soon. It was too fantastic a discovery to keep a secret. But maybe I wouldn't tell them right away. Maybe it could be my private place, just for a while anyway. Let Andrea and Vicki have their private "girl talk." Men could have secrets, too.

CHAPTER FOURTEEN

BACK AT THE COTTAGE I tied up the boat, trying to decide if I really wanted to take Josh fishing now. Afternoon fishing isn't my favorite. I could see Vicki and Andrea over at Marshalls' float. Vicki was sitting on the float talking to Brad. I don't think she even noticed I was back—she was slathering lotion on Brad's shoulders. I wondered what Mom would think if she saw that. Andrea saw me, though, and called over, "I'm coming in soon." I waved to her and started up the hill.

After the brightness outside, the inside of the cottage was so dim it took my eyes a minute to adjust. When they did, I saw a note on the kitchen table. "Josh and I are at grocery. Be home soon. Love, Mom." I was tired. I drank a glass of milk and then went into the main room and flopped down on the daybed. Something under the cover had a sharp corner, so I fished it out. It was Andrea's sketchbook, and it was open. She had been working on a drawing of the wicker rocker on the porch, the one we all fought over. Underneath it was written, "This is the rocker where Mom sat and rocked you two when you were babies. I used to climb up and join you, and Mom would say, "Careful, you'll squish them! Sometimes I thought that might be a good idea." It was Vicki's writing; she had taken calligraphy lessons, and her writing was a work of art. What was she doing, writing in Andrea's sketchbook?

Just then the screen door slammed and Andrea came in. When she saw what I was holding she took a deep breath that hissed through her clenched teeth. "Darn it! Give it to me!" she demanded. "Who said you could look in there without asking?"

"What's the big deal?" Maybe I raised my voice a little at this point, but I certainly didn't yell, the way she later said I did. "It was under the covers and it poked me, so I pulled it out. Just now. What's with you, anyway?"

"What's with me is that it's my sketchbook, and if I want to show it to you I will, and I don't want to, so keep your hands off."

I don't know if I was more shocked or angry at first, but as the seconds ticked by and Andrea stood there with her feet planted wide and a scowl on her face, anger took over.

So what if she'd made me a lunch; there was probably poison in it anyway.

The bad thing about being a boy is that I'm not allowed to hit a girl. If I were I'd have given Andrea a good sock right then. Instead I jumped up and kind of threw the sketchbook to her. She gave a little cry as it fell on the floor and one of the pages tore loose.

"Now see what you've done!" She started to cry as she bent to pick it up. Then she ran out of the cottage, sketchbook in her arms.

I just stood there, shaking my head. In a minute Vicki came in. "What did you do to Andrea?" she asked.

That was too much! I hadn't done anything, and here was Vicki blaming me because Andrea was acting like a brat.

"I didn't do anything," I said coldly. "Not that it's any of your business."

I hate fighting with people. Andrea came back in a while, her eyes and nose red. She went over to Vicki and said something I couldn't hear. Vicki nodded, and from then on they ignored me. When Mom got back and saw how things were, she gave me a puzzled look. I pretended I didn't see. The whole mess wasn't my fault, and I didn't see why I should be the one to explain. Instead I told Josh I'd give him a swimming lesson, but he said he wanted to catch crickets. When I offered to catch some too, he said, "No, it's my job. I can do it." I guess he didn't want my company either.

I hung around the kitchen for a while till Mom shooed me out, saying I'd ruin my appetite for supper. That was the last straw. "A guy can't do anything around here," I yelled. "I might as well have stayed away all day." I ran down to the boat. It was the wrong time of day for any serious fishing—the sun was too high—but at least on the lake nobody would be bugging me.

I pulled hard at the oars till the old boat skimmed along the water. Almost. You can't really make a rowboat skim. But I covered a good distance in a hurry. I anchored down by Lancers' Cove and threw out my line. I sat there and just watched the bobber riding along the wavelets. I had to squint because of the sun. A breeze tickled the back of my neck, and I felt my anger trickle away. It was too beautiful a day to stay mad at someone. The longer I sat there, the mellower I felt. I might even have considered apologizing to Andrea if I could figure out what I had to apologize for.

I fished for about two hours. I didn't catch anything, had only a couple of nibbles, and they weren't worth taking seriously. Finally I felt calm enough to go back. Besides, I was getting hungry.

Andrea was sitting on the pier, dangling her feet in the water, when I came in. I didn't know if she'd still be mad or not, so I didn't say anything. But as I was tying the boat up, she got to her feet and walked toward me, her bare feet leaving wet footprints on the pier behind her. "I'm sorry I got mad," she said. "But I don't want you looking in my sketchbook, okay?"

"Okay." What else could I say? I tried not to show her I was hurt, but I was. It seemed like all summer—ever since we got here, anyway—she and Vicki had been hanging out together. They were always whispering and doing things without me. I knew Andrea didn't like to fish, but last summer she'd helped dig for worms, and sometimes she'd gone out on the boat with me so she could sketch the shoreline. I liked having her with me. All she'd ask was for me to row by the water lilies on the way home so she could pick a couple. But she hadn't been out in the boat with me even once this summer. Well, I wasn't going to show I cared.

Now she stood looking at me, rubbing her wet toe along the edge of the pier. "I just wrote a letter to Dad," she said. "Do you want to add a message?"

"No."

"Have you written to him at all?"

"No, and I'm not going to."

"Okay. Your choice." She sounded just like Mom when she said that.

I watched her go down the length of the pier and start up toward the cottage. I thought about calling her back and saying I'd write a line or two if it would make her happy, but I decided against it. It was about time somebody tried to see things from my point of view. Why did I always have to be the reasonable one?

At dinner we all just sort of sat there. Mom thinks dinner should be a "sociable occasion," so she tried to get conversation going. "How was the island exploration, Kyle? Find anything interesting?"

"Not a lot," I muttered. That was only a half lie, I thought.

"You haven't forgotten your promise, have you?"

"Promise?"

"Tuesday afternoon, around four."

"Oh, that. Josh, you want to go fishing with me tomorrow afternoon?"

"Uh-huh." He nodded vigorously, adding, "I need the practice."

"Practice? What are you practicing for?"

"For when you and Mr. Butler take me some morning."

"Where'd you get that idea?" I asked. I hadn't said anything to him about Tom's offer, and I didn't think Mom had either. I looked at him. He was carefully removing bones from his perch. He's always worried he'll overlook one and get it stuck in his throat. I think once I told him he would, just joking, and I scared him for life.

"Mr. Butler told me. We saw him at the grocery this afternoon. He gave me an ice-cream bar."

"How many did he eat?" I asked with a laugh.

Mom gave me a disapproving look and said, "I don't see why that should concern you, Kyle."

And then Vicki had to join in. "You sniggered!" she exclaimed. "Finally I know what a snigger sounds like. Authors are always writing that someone or other 'gave a snigger,' but that's the first one I ever heard."

"I didn't snigger, I just laughed. Didn't I?" I looked around for support, but I didn't get any. It wasn't my night for the dishes, so I wadded up my paper napkin, threw it on the table, pushed away my chair and left. No one called me back.

As I lay in bed that night, I thought what a lousy ending it was to what had begun as a great day. But at least I'd found the cabin. It was pretty cool to think that I might be the only person who knew it was there. Aside from whoever built it, I mean. I just might start spending all my free time there—it didn't look as if anyone here would miss me.

CHAPTER FIFTEEN

THE NEXT MORNING TOM BUTLER didn't go fishing. He wasn't waiting when I got to his cottage, so I had to knock, and he came to the door in pajama bottoms and an undershirt. "Not going today. Feeling poorly," was his only explanation.

"Will you be all right?" I asked.

He grunted what was probably "yes" and turned away.

Just like that, I had a free morning. Of course that meant less money the next time he paid me. Darn. What now? Fish as usual? Go out to the island? For some reason the thought of a morning by myself didn't appeal to me today. Walking back to the cottage, I tried to figure out why not. Usually I like being alone. Then the eeriest thing happened. It was like I suddenly heard Dad's voice whispering to me. "Mend your fences," he said. I could almost feel his breath on my ear. I knew he wasn't there, of course—I didn't turn around to look or anything—but somehow I caught myself starting to cry. I hadn't heard Dad use that expression for years, not since I was a little kid sulking around the house after a fight with Andrea or Vicki. "You need to mend your fences," he'd say. "C'mon, cowboy." And after I'd made up with whoever, I'd feel better.

What good was a father who was only a voice? I stood still on the road while the dumb tears rolled, waiting for them to stop—no way was anyone going to see me cry. When I was sure I was through, I started walking again. Then I had an inspiration. I would take Josh out this morning instead of waiting till afternoon. The fishing would be better now, and he might like getting up early for a change.

Back at the cottage, I wrote a note for Mom. "Took Josh fishing. Back for breakfast." Then I crept into the main room and, reaching up into the top bunk, gently shook Josh awake.

Other people—Mom, for instance—sometimes wake up groggy. Not Josh. He's wide awake in an instant. "Get your clothes on," I whispered. "We're going fishing."

"Now?"

"Now."

"Oh, boy!"

While he was getting dressed, I made a couple of

bologna sandwiches. I didn't usually eat anything till I came back in for breakfast, but Josh was always hungry, and I didn't want him bugging me a half hour after we got out. I poured us both a bowl of cereal—cornflakes for me and sugary stuff for him. I had them both ready when he came out, but for some reason today he didn't want the sugary stuff. "I want the cereal you eat," he said.

He started shoving it down so quickly I finally said, "Slow down! The fish aren't going anywhere."

"How come we're going this morning? Is Mr. Butler going too?" he asked.

"Not so loud. You'll wake Mom and the girls. Tom doesn't feel good this morning, so it's just you and me."

Down at the lake he put on his life jacket and carried the bait to the boat while I got our poles ready. "Is that my pole?" he asked. "Can I have a green and yellow bobber?"

"Better stick to red and white," I advised. "They're easier to see."

When we got in the boat, I let him row. "Hear the woodpecker?" I whispered as we cleared Marshalls' float. "He wakes me up every morning."

"Where is he?" Josh whispered back.

"I don't know." I shrugged. "Back behind the cottage someplace, I guess."

"No, he isn't!" Josh forgot to whisper. "He's right over there! Look!"

He pointed, and I looked, and sure enough, there was the red head high on the trunk of the hickory that grew halfway down the hill. "Good eye!" I congratulated him.

Pretty soon Josh got tired of rowing, so we carefully switched seats, and I took us the rest of the way. I was headed for the drop-off on the northern side of the island.

"We're not going to be feeding babies this morning," I cautioned him. "You probably won't get many bites, but when you do, it'll be a keeper."

I anchored us about thirty feet from the island. The anchors went down, down, down, so I knew we were beyond the drop-off. I passed the worms to Josh and unwound his pole. I'd brought him the short one Gram had always used. It looked like it would be just right for him.

"I'm going to get a real fat worm," he said, digging down into the dirt. He probably rejected six before he selected a fat, wiggly one and began to bait his hook. "Hold still, won't you?" he fussed at the worm.

"What's the matter, Josh? Won't he behave?" I joked.

Josh has been fishing before, and he's a pretty athletic little kid, so he doesn't have any trouble casting his line where he wants it. The trouble is, no sooner does the bobber settle down than he decides he'd rather have it someplace else. That was my goal for the morning, to get him to leave his line in till he had a good reason to move it.

He was hunched over, staring at his bobber, while I readied my pole. "I think I've got a bite," he murmured. "Look, Kyle!"

I looked. The bobber was riding the water peacefully.

"That's just the motion of the waves."

"Oh."

I threw my line where I could keep an eye on both bobbers at once.

Five, maybe ten, minutes went by, and suddenly Josh jerked his pole.

"What was that for?"

"I thought I had a bite."

"When you have a bite out here, you'll know it. Your bobber will go all the way under. You don't pull until then."

I knew I was testing his patience, but if he was going to go out with Tom Butler, he couldn't be pulling his line in all the time and chattering away too.

Pretty soon he said, "Kyle?"

"Hmm?"

"Do I have a bite?"

"No. Yes, yes, you do! Pull!"

He gave his pole a yank. "Careful! Keep him underwater!" I watched as Josh pulled in. "Bring him to the side of the boat. Keep your line taut!"

As the fish came alongside, I grabbed his line and pulled up. "How about that, Josh! A bluegill. Big one, too."

He was so excited he almost started to stand. "Sit down! Do you want to capsize us?" I snapped. He sat, and I took the bluegill off the hook and slipped it into the live-sack. "Didn't even get your worm."

"I'm going to cast out the same place. Maybe there's another one there," Josh said. It took him three casts to get the bobber exactly where he wanted it, but I didn't fuss. I've done the same thing myself sometimes.

It's a good thing we caught that one, because from then on the morning was dead. After a bit I got out the sandwiches. "I like mustard on mine," he complained.

"I forgot. At least you have something to eat."

I'll say this for Josh. He was trying real hard. He hardly pulled his line in at all. I remember when I was little, wondering if some fish had taken my bait when I wasn't looking, if I had an empty hook floating deep in the green water.

The boat rocked gently as we sat there, and now and then I looked over at the island and kind of smiled to myself. I knew what was hidden in there among the trees.

I wondered why someone would build in the middle, where you'd have no water view. Then I realized. If you couldn't see the lake, no one on the lake could see you. If you wanted a place to be alone, you wouldn't want to be in full view of every boat on the water. Was that what the person who built it wanted, a place to hide away? What kind of people wanted that—hermits, criminals, spies . . . ? I was letting my mind wander when Josh spoke so quietly I wasn't even sure I'd heard him.

"If you go again, will you take me along, Kyle?"

I looked at him. He was staring at the island with a funny look on his face, sort of like he was looking at a giant birthday cake and waiting for someone to light the candles.

"There's not much there," I told him.

"You don't know. You prob'ly didn't see the whole island. Maybe there's something you didn't find. Maybe there's a pirate treasure hidden someplace. Or maybe a gorilla or something escaped from a zoo, and it's living there."

"There aren't any zoos around here." I couldn't keep from smiling as I said that. It was the sort of thing I used to think at his age. Maybe Josh and I were more alike than I'd thought.

"Gorillas can travel a long way." His jaw was set the way

it was when he was driving for a soccer goal. I let him have the last word, and we fished on in silence. A half hour or so later, I decided he'd been patient enough, so I told him to bring his line in. "We'll pull up anchor and go down by the channel," I said.

"Yeah, maybe all the fish are down there." He sounded more eager than I expected. Maybe catching that one fish had awakened the fisherman in him. He'd never seemed this interested before.

We went down by the channel and had no luck there, either. But Josh didn't complain, didn't fuss to go back in. Maybe he was old enough to go with Tom and me after all.

When my stomach began to think about breakfast, I told Josh I was ready to head back in. "Can I leave my line in the lake while we row back?" he begged. "Maybe a fish will see my worm and chase it."

"Sure," I said with a little chuckle, "but I wouldn't count on it."

When we got back, Josh scrambled out of the boat and grabbed the live-sack. "I'm going to take my fish up to show Mom," he said.

"First, you're going to help put things away." I handed him his pole and the bait can.

"But I want to fish off the end of the dock. Do we have

126

to put stuff away right now? Can't I fish? Just till breakfast is ready?"

I stared at him in amazement. What a change. He really had caught the fishing bug! "Sure," I said. "If you need help, call me. Keep your life jacket on, remember."

Up in the cottage, I was surprised to find that Mom and Vicki and Andrea had already finished breakfast. Vicki was making beds, Andrea was sweeping the floor, and Mom was finishing up the dishes. "You and Josh will have to get something in a hurry," she said. "Someone's coming to look at the cottage in about a half hour."

I groaned. "Why so early?" I asked.

"I've no idea," she said with a smile. "But no matter when they planned to come, you wouldn't want them. Call Josh."

"Okay," I said. I hesitated. "Mom? What if I could find a way to pay the taxes? Then we wouldn't have to sell, would we?"

"Where would you get that kind of money?"

"Well, I might. Would we? Have to sell, then?"

"I don't know, Kyle. I really don't. I told you. If we sell the cottage, I can put the money away in the college funds. It wouldn't cover all the costs, of course, but it would help. And I'm just afraid that as you kids grow older it will be harder and harder to make use of the cottage. It won't be just Vicki and Josh—you and Andrea will have activities, too, things that will make you want to spend more of the summer in Cincinnati."

"Not me. I'll always want to come here."

"You think so now, but . . ."

"I know so."

I guess I sounded kind of belligerent, because she pressed her lips tight for a minute, then said, "Well, there's no point in talking about it. They'll be here in half an hour, and I want you and Josh out of the kitchen by then."

When Josh came up from the pier, he had the live-sack in his hands. Mom peered in. "Wow!" she said. "That's an impressive bluegill. Wait here and I'll get the camera. We'll send a picture to your dad."

Josh looked from her to me, then back to her. "Naw," he said. "He doesn't need to see it."

Mom closed her eyes and wrinkled her forehead. "I think he'd like to," she told Josh gently.

"You can take one picture," he conceded. "Maybe I'll give it to him someday."

Mom glared at me like this was my fault. But I didn't have anything to do with it, I thought. Josh had a mind of his own, didn't he?

* * *

I was sorting through a box of old bobbers and stuff down on the pier when Dave Becker's car drove up. Another car came right behind, a Chevy wagon like ours, only a more expensive model, with wood paneling on the sides and back. As soon as the cars stopped, the door of the second car opened, and two kids about Josh's age or a little younger hopped out. Their little-kid voices carried clearly. "Can we go down by the lake while you look at the cottage? Can we, Mom?"

A hesitation. Then, doubtfully, "I guess it will be all right. Don't go out on the pier, though, and don't get too close to the water."

I had to laugh. She sounded just like Mom—wanting the kids to have fun, but worrying. I watched them skip down the steps. The one in front, a boy, had curly, copper-colored hair and a face full of freckles. The girl behind him had hair so red it was almost orange, and even more freckles. They went running across the grass right to the foot of the pier. There they stopped and looked at me.

"Is this your pier?" the boy asked.

"Mmm-hmm."

"And the cottage, is it yours, too?" The little girl was trying to stand as close to the pier as her brother did, but he was blocking her way.

"Yes, the cottage is ours, too."

"Why do you want to sell it? If we get a cottage by a lake we'll never, ever sell it," she said.

I thought about telling her I didn't want to sell, but I figured it wasn't any of her business, so I just shrugged.

"Is the water deep here?" the boy asked.

"Only about a foot or two here, but it's over your head at the end of the pier."

"That's what we want," the little girl told me. "The last cottage we looked at, the water was deep right at the shore. Mom said it would make her too nervous to live there. Maybe she'll like your cottage."

"I hope she won't," I said under my breath, but the little girl had sharp ears. "Why do you hope she won't?" she asked. "Don't you like us?"

I couldn't help grinning at that. "How can I not like you? I don't know you," I said. "I just don't want anyone to buy the cottage."

"Not even if we give you a lot of money?"

"Not even then." They both looked so disappointed, I felt mean. "It's not up to me, though," I said.

"Who's it up to?"

"My mom."

They looked at each other, and then they both turned

back toward the cottage. "We'll go look at your cottage," the little boy said.

They ran across the grass and started up the hill. Halfway to the cottage, the little girl turned around. "If we buy your cottage, you can come and stay with us sometimes," she called.

"Thanks," I said. I said it sarcastically, but quietly enough, I hoped, that she couldn't hear me. I knew she thought she was being nice, but this whole business brought out the worst in me. I watched them continue up the steps. If I didn't want to keep the cottage so badly, they'd be people I'd want to sell it to. They looked like the kind of family who could have fun here.

This time I didn't go up to the cottage while Mr. Becker was showing it. I wanted to, but I had promised Mom I would stay out of the way. "Actually," she'd said, "I guess it's just as well if you don't go into town with us. Then if Dave has questions or a message for me, he'll have someone to talk to."

So I just sat there, listening to the breeze-driven waves slap the shore, looking out at the island. Three boats were out off the western point. I wondered how they were doing. Above me the woodpecker was tapping. Down at the channel end of the lake, a crow cawed. It's not just the cottage I'd miss, I realized. I'd miss the lake itself. I knew there were lots of other lakes; southern Michigan was rich with them. But this was the one I knew. I knew the exact place the sun came up each morning. I knew where to fish when it was clear and when it was cloudy. I knew where the water lilies grew, and I knew how to pole through the reeds in the channel. I'd been learning this lake since I was just a little boy, but there was more of it still to discover. I'd hardly ever been all the way down to the eastern end. This was the summer Dad was going to show me how to use the motor; this was the summer the two of us were going to fish Pringle's Cove, where there was supposed to be an old catfish bigger than you could believe. This was my lake.

The sound of footsteps on the pier startled me. It was Dave Becker. "Tell your mom I'll try to call this afternoon," he said.

"Do they like it?"

"Hard to tell. The kids sure do. I'll keep you posted."

I watched him stride back up the hill, taking the steps two at a time. For a minute, I hated him, even though I knew he was just doing his job.

After they left I went back up to the cottage and lay

down on the porch with the book I was reading. It was peaceful, so peaceful I fell asleep and didn't wake up till I heard our car door slam.

Mom came in the kitchen door. "Kyle?"

"Out here," I called.

She came through the main room and stood in the doorway. "Well?" she asked. "Did Dave say anything?"

"He said he'd call."

"Did he say whether they liked it?"

"He didn't say," I said. I could have told her the kids did, but what difference does it make what kids want? I kept still, and she went back into the kitchen.

I didn't know what to do with myself that afternoon. I finished my book and played a game of Scrabble with Vicki, which was very nice of me because Vicki beats everyone at Scrabble. That was two mended fences, I thought. When the game was over, Vicki said she was going to find Andrea and Josh to go swimming. I thought about it, but I didn't feel like swimming. Besides, I was staying away from the Marshalls. I'd joined them down at their float one day, and they were just as bad as I remembered. Plus they'd each grown about ten inches, and somehow this made them think they'd gained a year or two on me as well. I wasn't going to be treated like a little kid by anyone. So even though swimming sounded kind of like fun, I decided instead I'd go see if Tom Butler was feeling any better.

"C'mon in," he called when I knocked at his kitchen door for the second time that day. He was sitting at the table, a plate of ham and potatoes and green beans in front of him. There was a big stack of bread, a stick of butter, and a little pitcher of honey on the table, too. An open quart of milk stood by a full glass.

"I came to find out if you were feeling better," I said.

"Fine now. Just a touch of indigestion."

"Indigestion?" I asked, glancing at the table.

He grunted. "I said I was better."

"Oh. Well, I guess you'll want to go out tomorrow?"

"Far as I know. You want to take your brother along with us?"

"You sure you want him? I know he'd like to go, but sometimes he can be a pest."

He let out a sound that I think was a laugh. "A pest, hmm? Just like most boys, I suspect. Tell him if he don't behave, we'll pitch him overboard."

"Okay, then. I'll see you tomorrow." I started to go, then turned around. "Say, Mr. Butler—I mean, Tom. Do you know, did anybody ever live on the island?"

"Nah," he said, shoving half a slice of bread into his mouth and chewing vigorously. He swallowed before going on. "You couldn't live out there. What would you use for heat in the winter? And drinking water, that would be a problem."

"I hadn't thought of that," I said. "I was just wondering, that's all."

I let myself out the door and headed back for the cottage. So Tom Butler didn't know someone had a cabin on the island. And if he didn't know, was there anyone else who might?

As I got close to the cottage, I saw Andrea ahead of me, strolling along with her head down, her sketchbook under her arm. I thought I might as well catch up with her. Things had been kind of prickly between us lately, but I couldn't stay mad at her, and I didn't think she could stay mad at me.

I hurried, and she heard me coming and turned her head. "Hey, Kyle," she said.

"Hey, yourself."

"Those people this morning?"

"What about them?"

"You sounded funny when you were talking to Mom. Didn't you like them?"

"I only met the kids. They were cute. And they want a cottage real bad. I don't know what their parents thought about it."

"Do you suppose we'll get lucky and no one will want to buy it?"

"I don't know." I kicked a little stone, then bent over and picked up another. I pitched it at a nearby sapling. Bull's-eye! "I'm beginning to lose hope. I asked Mom, if we could pay the taxes, then would we still have to sell? I didn't tell her about the plan, I just said, what if? But she wouldn't say we could keep it. She said she'd have to think."

"Do you think maybe we should write Dad?"

"What for? If he didn't care enough to come up here, why would he care if we have to sell it?"

"I guess you're right." She sounded discouraged, and I felt lousy for putting her in a bad mood, too.

"I thought you were going swimming this afternoon," I said, hoping to cheer her up.

"I had something I wanted to do first."

Again. Just like a door slamming in my face—"something I wanted to do." Not, "I wanted to sketch the Petersens' cottage" or "I thought I'd . . ." Well, cripes, what had she been doing? Not that I cared. If she wanted to keep her secrets, let her. But I bet she'd tell Vicki.

Before I could get really mad again, she said, "I'm going to swim now, though. Want to come?"

"Sure." At least I'm good enough to swim with, I thought but didn't say.

Maybe some of my anger sounded in my voice. She gave me a long, serious look, like she was trying to read my mind. "You don't have to if you don't want," she said.

But suddenly that was what I wanted to do more than anything else. Just dive into the water, swim out to the float and let the water wash away all my worries. Why let the Marshalls or anyone else spoil my fun?

"Beat you to the cottage," I told Andrea.

She laughed. "In your dreams, slowpoke," and we both took off.

Fence number three was a hard one to mend, I thought as I ran.

CHAPTER SIXTEEN

I'D NEVER FOUND TOM much for laughing, not until the day Josh went fishing with us. But that morning he laughed a lot, and he probably talked twice as much as usual. For some reason, Josh affected Tom the way Mom did—both of them seemed to loosen his tongue. Tom even told Josh a riddle: "What's gray, has four legs, and a trunk?"

Of course Josh guessed, "An elephant."

"No," said Tom with a perfectly straight face, "a mouse on vacation."

I didn't let Josh row. I figured there'd be too much weight in the boat. Besides, Tom suggested going almost all the way to the channel, down where the reeds stood high above the surface. There was plenty of bird life in the reeds and enough babies in the water to keep Josh's bobber busy. "Don't want you to get bored," Tom told Josh.

"I won't," Josh said, and I believed him. As soon as

they'd gotten back from town yesterday, Josh had gone straight out to the pier with his bait and his pole, and he hadn't left until Vicki suggested swimming.

I had warned Josh before we left that he wasn't supposed to chatter to Mr. Butler, and he was positively not to complain about anything. As it turned out, I needn't have worried. Tom Butler was going to make sure that Josh had a good day. We'd hardly got our lines in the water when Tom reached into the big bag he'd brought along and pulled out a bag of little Milky Ways.

"Have a candy bar," he invited us.

"No, thanks." I shook my head—I don't eat candy that early in the day. "It'll make you thirsty," I warned Josh as he took one.

"Thought of that," Tom said. "I brought something to wash it down." It was pop, of course. I noticed he hadn't brought along a toothbrush, which Josh's teeth could use after all that sugar.

How come Tom could eat candy and cookies all the time and not get sick? It didn't make sense. But nothing made sense this summer. It should be Dad here telling jokes with Josh and giving him fishing tips, like how to decide where to set his bobber, things like that.

But Dad wasn't here, and since he wasn't, it was nice of

Tom to give Josh so much attention. I didn't blame Josh for eating it up. Once he tried to tell Tom a joke. He took a long time, because he kept getting mixed up and saying, "No, I mean . . ." and backing up a little. But Tom listened patiently, and when Josh said, "No, that's not right, I meant . . ." for about the eighth time, Tom winked at me and smiled over Josh's head. It was kind of like we shared a grown-up secret. I was surprised at the nice warm feeling that gave me.

But as the sun rose higher and the morning wore on, I started to get seriously annoyed. Tom had prepared for this fishing trip as if it were going to last days instead of hours. I never saw so much junk food in my life. And Josh, of course, thought it was great. Everything Tom offered him he ate.

I tried to discourage Josh from eating any more. "You'll get a stomachache," I warned, sounding just like Gram.

"Leave him be, Kyle," Tom said. "He's a growing boy. A few treats won't hurt him."

So the two of them kept eating and fishing and eating and fishing while I sat there feeling helpless. It was as if Tom knew ahead of time what a sweet tooth Josh has. I tried shaking my head at Josh and frowning when Tom offered him a second candy bar. After all, they'd already eaten peanut butter and jelly sandwiches and a whole bag of potato chips. But Josh just ignored me.

On top of everything else, in between bites Josh caught a really mammoth smallmouth bass, and he brought it in without any help, except for the netting at the end. You think that didn't make him proud? He wasn't about to pay any attention to me after that.

So all I could do was sit there fuming. I thought Tom would never say it was time to go in, but he did, and to my amazement he said it just like always, "Must be nine o'clock. Time for breakfast."

After we pulled in, on the way up to Tom's cottage, I lagged behind and pulled Josh's arm. "He's going to ask us to stay for breakfast," I whispered. "You can't be hungry still."

"Sure I can," Josh said with a grin.

Later, sitting at the table with a tall stack of pancakes in front of Josh, a smaller one in front of me, and a giant one in front of him, Tom looked over at me. Something of what I was thinking must have been showing on my face, because he said quietly, "Don't be a killjoy, Kyle. Eating ain't a sin."

I was glad to get out of there that day. Josh and I walked home side by side, and I had absolutely no pity when Josh said, "My tummy doesn't feel so good."

Later on, though, when he threw up, I wasn't as mad at him as I was at Tom. He shouldn't have encouraged Josh. When Mom started asking Josh about what he had eaten that might have made him sick, I just exploded. "It's not what he ate, it's how much he ate," I said. I told her about all the snacking and the big breakfast. "Tom says eating's not a sin," I said. "But there's some sin that has to do with eating—I remember learning that in Sunday School."

"Gluttony," Mom said quietly. "But it's not for us to judge."

"Why not?" I asked. "Didn't he make Josh sick?"

"Josh made himself sick," she said. "Tom didn't stuff food down Josh's throat."

"But you should see the way Tom eats," I raged. "It's sick. No wonder he's as big as a whale."

"Tom Butler has been good to you," Mom said. Her eyes darkened, so I knew she was getting angry. "That's no way to talk!"

I couldn't understand her. Her own son was sicker than a dog, and she was defending the man who'd made him that way. Well, I didn't care what she thought. I was mad at Tom Butler, and it would be a long time before I'd forgive him.

Josh went in to lie down on Mom's bed then. I hadn't been back long enough to wonder where Andrea and Vicki were, but now I heard Vicki call to someone, "See you out there!" and she and Andrea came through the kitchen door.

"Hi, Kyle! You guys have a good time?" Vicki asked.

She poured a dipper of water into one of the paper cups Mom kept by the water bucket. Andrea went straight to the fridge and pulled out a slice of cheese—Andrea doesn't eat much, but she eats often. She sat down with Mom and me.

"Aren't you coming?" Vicki asked Andrea, throwing away her empty cup.

"I may come out later—you don't have to wait for me."

"'Kay." Vicki went into the main room.

"Where's Vicki going?" I asked.

"Brad and Jeff asked us to come swimming," Andrea said. "Vicki is so glad she bought that new suit."

"Aren't you going, too?" Mom asked.

Andrea shook her head. "I don't think I should."

"Because . . ." Mom prompted, cocking her head the way she does when she wants more information.

"No reason," Andrea said. "I don't know why I put it like that." I haven't been Andrea's twin all this time without knowing how to tell when she's trying to fool someone. She had a reason, all right. She just didn't want to explain it to Mom. She got up from the table before Mom could ask anything more. "Can I take the rowboat, Kyle? I thought I'd row down to where the ducklings are, try to sketch them."

"Sure, take it," I said.

I thought maybe she'd ask me to go with her, but she didn't. Instead, Mom told me, "If you're going to be here, maybe I'll run into Cass and see if there's any mail. I think Josh fell asleep."

Andrea left, Mom left, and Vicki'd already gone. I wandered into the main room and stood in front of the table where Gram's old books were stacked. I found one called *White Fang* by Jack London. I thought I'd heard of him, and the title sounded exciting, so I took it out on the porch and lay down to read a little. I had maybe a half hour of quiet before I heard someone coming up the steps. I raised up to look through the screens. It was Vicki. She was moving slower than usual, looking down at her feet, so her hair fell like a curtain and hid her face from me.

She opened the porch door and started past me to the main room. "I thought you'd be out at the float all afternoon," I said.

"Brad and Jeff decided they'd had enough sun," Vicki said, and then she added kind of under her breath, "since Andrea didn't come back out."

"Andrea? Why should she make a difference?"

Vicki sighed. "She's the only one the guys pay attention to. They tell her jokes, they offer to take her water-skiing. And while she wasn't there this afternoon, they spent the whole time asking me if she had a boyfriend—stuff like that."

"A boyfriend?" The thought of it almost made me laugh. "What makes them think she'd have a boyfriend already? She's too busy with her art stuff."

"Oh, Kyle, you're so—so blind, sometimes. Have you looked at Andrea lately?"

"What do you mean? I look at her all the time. We're together every day, aren't we?"

"Well, if you'd really looked, you'd have noticed—she's beautiful. You two have always been the good-looking ones, with your black hair, and those blue eyes, and now . . ."

Vicki trailed off, like she was thinking of something she didn't want to say. She didn't look very happy. I felt like she was hoping I'd say something.

"You're pretty too, Vick," I told her.

"If you like streaky blond hair with no body to it," she said. Suddenly she grinned, and just like that, her mood seemed to change. "Anyway," she said, "who cares what a couple of dumb boys think? Do you know neither of them has read *Catcher in the Rye*?"

I hadn't either, but I didn't say so.

"I'm going to get a pop and then go lie out on the pier a bit. Unless you want me to stay up here with Josh."

"You go on. I'll just keep reading."

I'm not usually much of a reader, but this book was really good. I kept turning pages. After a while I heard Andrea's voice down by the pier, so I knew she was back. Josh woke up and came out on the porch. "Can I go down and fish from the pier?" he asked.

"As long as Andrea and Vicki are down there and you wear your life jacket," I told him. He looked completely recovered to me. He left then, and I lay back down on my bed. The cottage dozed around me, and I was completely, utterly happy. Until.

I didn't pay much attention when the car door slammed. I heard Mrs. Morley call, "Dorrie? Dave Becker phoned. He'd like you to call him."

I hoped Mr. Becker didn't want to bring someone new to look at the cottage. But it wasn't that. It was worse. Mom came back with her eyes shining. "You know the family who was here yesterday, Kyle? They liked the cottage. They made a good offer."

I sat up so fast I knocked my book to the floor.

"You didn't take it?"

"I did."

"Just like that? Without talking it over with us?"

"Kyle, there wasn't any point in talking. It's a fair offer, and we need to sell."

"I told you I'd never forgive you!" I shouted. "And I never will!"

I ran out of the cottage and down to the pier. Ignoring Vicki and Andrea and Josh, I got into the rowboat. Mom was calling to me, but I paid no attention—just grabbed my life jacket and bait can, loosened the rope, and shoved off. I didn't know where I was going. My fishing pole was in the boat, where I'd put it when we came back from Tom's. I didn't know if I'd want to fish, but I'd let them think I did. Who cared about me anyway? Mom had gotten what she wanted, and Vicki and Andrea and Josh didn't really love the cottage the way I did. Give them a few days, and they'd be used to the idea that it was no longer ours. Not me, though. I'd never get used to it.

I ended up going to the island, of course. I guess I'd known I would even before I got in the boat. I headed straight out there. When I got up close, instead of anchoring out in the open the way I did before, I pulled the boat in under some overhanging trees so that it was kind of hidden. I didn't want anyone on the lake—the Marshalls, say—to see it and guess someone was out here.

This time it was easier to find my way to the cabin. When I got there, the first thing I did was prop open the door and open the window as wide as it would go. I took the blanket and pillow off the cot and carried them outside, where I draped the blanket over a bush. I didn't see a good place to put the pillow, so I just dropped it on top of some vines on the ground. I hoped the sun and wind would get rid of some of that musty smell. After that I went back in and grabbed the broom. Might as well get the worst job over with first. I swept every inch of that cabin, walls and all. I got rid of cobwebs and spiderwebs and the leaves and twigs that fell from the sill when I opened the window. I took off my T-shirt and used it to dust the crates and the cans. When I finished, a good look at the shirt convinced me not to put it on again.

After I'd done all that, I brought the blanket and pillow back in. I spread the blanket on the cot, tossed on the pillow, then lay down. The wool was scratchy on my bare back, and the pillow still smelled musty, but all in all it wasn't bad. I clasped my hands behind my neck, crossed my ankles, closed my eyes. Maybe I'd just stay here on the island and eat from the cans till I ran out of food. How long would that take? I wouldn't, of course. I knew Mom. The first hint of darkness and she'd be wild with worry if I wasn't back. Still, I liked thinking about staying. . . .

I must have fallen asleep then, I guess, because when I opened my eyes the dimmed light told me it was getting late. I lay there a minute longer, letting the reality of losing the cottage sink in. It was strange—my anger seemed to be gone, and in its place was a kind of sadness that I didn't think would leave me soon.

It was almost dark by the time I got back in. I'd missed lunch and supper, but I wasn't hungry. As I tied the boat up, I noticed Mom sitting at the bottom of the steps. I wasn't in the mood to talk, so I put away my pole and bait, then started to go past her up the steps. Glancing down at her, though, I was surprised to see what looked like tear stains on her cheeks.

"Mom? Have you been crying?"

"Maybe a little. Go on up. I'll be there soon."

"Why were you crying?" I sat down on the step beside her and put my arm around her shoulders. "Did Dad call?"

"No, this has nothing to do with your dad. I'm just sad, that's all."

"What are you sad about?"

She gave an angry sniff and turned to look at me. "About the cottage, of course. Did you think I wouldn't care? I grew up with this cottage, Kyle. Every room is full of memories of my mom and dad. First the house in Cassopolis, now this. Soon my memories will have no place to stay."

I didn't say anything. How could I? I'd been thinking

only of me, of how I'd miss the cottage. I'd never dreamed that Mom might feel the same way. I wasn't ready to forgive her, though. If she'd tried a little harder, maybe she could have figured out a way to save it. I wouldn't have given up that easily. Still . . .

"Want a cup of coffee?" I asked. "I'll fix you one."

She smiled and shook her head, then lit a cigarette. "No, but if you'll spend some time with Josh, I'll appreciate it. He's done nothing but mope around since you left. Most of the time he's been sitting on the pier, looking at the island, waiting for you to get back."

"He knew I was on the island?"

"He watched you go, guessed you'd end up there. He's a lot like you, Kyle."

So I went on up to the cottage. The lights inside were on, and it looked so comfortable and inviting, I had to swallow hard. Dad, I thought. This was all your fault. How could you do this to us?

CHAPTER SEVENTEEN

JULY 14, FIVE DAYS BEFORE my birthday. Two weeks since Dave Becker had pulled up the "For Sale" sign and replaced it with one that said "Sold." I had to pass it four times a day—going to and from Clyde's with my worms, and to and from Tom's. Every time I went by, I kicked a little dust up on it. It had rained some the day before, and as I left for Tom's that morning I noticed that the dust had turned to mud, so now the word *Sold* was hardly visible. Didn't bother me at all.

The morning was hot and muggy, kind of unsettled, with the sky in the east an orange-ish red. After so many beautiful days, I felt I shouldn't complain, but when my T-shirt started to stick to me on the way, I knew it was going to be a scorcher.

"Morning," I said when Tom came out his kitchen door.

He grunted. "Hotter'n Hades, isn't it?"

We didn't say anything more. Things had changed between Tom and me since the day Josh had gone out with us. I wasn't even quite sure why I kept fishing with him. The money was nice, but it wasn't any real use anymore. Maybe I just felt I should stay with it because I'd promised. And because I knew him well enough now to understand how awful it would be for him if he couldn't fish.

But I was still mad about the way he'd stuffed Josh with food. We'd never talked much, but now we talked less, and I hadn't stayed for breakfast since. If Tom wondered why, he didn't let on. To my relief, he hadn't asked me anything about the cottage. The first day the sign went up, he told me, "Sorry about your cottage, Kyle. A shame." And that's all he'd ever said.

I got the boat ready, Tom got in, and we shoved off. "Where to?" I asked him.

"By the bar, west of the island. They'll be deep today."

We anchored in the deepest part of the lake. The anchors went down so far that for a minute I was afraid we'd run out of rope. We threw out our lines and settled in. Two or three other boats were within hailing distance, but no one called over; they just acknowledged our presence with a nod of the head or a slight wave. The sun slipped up over the horizon, hot and red. As it climbed higher, my eyes began to water now and then. I had one of Grandpa's old fishing caps on, and I pulled the brim down a little.

Our bobbers sat quiet on the almost motionless water. A dragonfly lit on mine and rested there. Then, without warning, Tom's bobber disappeared. He jerked, then began pulling. His pole bent toward the water. His line kept going around in circles, but he kept it taut and gradually drew it closer. What he finally brought in was one of the biggest bluegills I'd ever seen. It must have weighed a pound if it weighed an ounce.

He held it up for a minute, and from the closest boat a voice called out across the water. "Guess now you'll be down at Clyde's bragging all week long, Tom."

And Tom called back, "You're just jealous, Hap."

He was slipping it into the live-sack when my bobber took a brief dive and then went down for good. That began the craziest morning of fishing I'd ever seen. Everything was biting—bass, bluegills, sunfish, perch. You'd hardly throw your line in before something took your bait. We were so busy, we didn't pay any attention as one by one the boats around us departed. When a breeze came up and a cloud moved across the sun, all it meant to me was that I was a little cooler. Tom, too, paid no attention to anything but the fishing. That's why the first roll of thunder startled me so. I looked up, and the sky was almost black. The wind grabbed my hat, and the hat went sailing away. A crack sounded off to the west, and I saw a flash of lightning streak down toward the water. The thunder rolled again, and as if a giant dishpan was overturned on us, the rain poured down.

"Blast it, I should have been paying attention," Tom shouted over the wind. We brought in our lines and began to pull up the anchors. But they were down so far! It seemed to take forever. Finally we had them back in the boat. I started toward the middle, but Tom motioned me to stay where I was. "I'll row," he shouted. He raised himself to his feet, took a step, and then it happened. A wave slapped us sideways, his foot caught in the wet anchor rope, and he lurched forward. His arms flew out to catch himself, but the sides of the boat were slippery, and his hands couldn't save him. He fell heavily, his forehead hitting the side of the boat with a thump I could hear over the wind, and then he lay there, motionless.

"Tom? Tom, are you all right?" My voice rose in a kind of screech.

He didn't stir. "Tom, get up! Get up!" I called again, and I know there was a sob in my voice. Crouching low, holding the sides of the boat, I moved forward till I was looking down at him, at his gray hair and the bald spot on the top of his head, at the thick shoulders and middle. He was lying on his stomach across the center seat, his upper body slumping down into the bottom of the boat. The rain soaked us both, and the wind was pushing the boat across the water. Somehow I pulled Tom farther toward the bow. If the rain hadn't made everything slippery, I don't think I could have done it. How much did he weigh? Three hundred pounds? More? And it was all dead weight. I pulled until only his legs were still on the center seat. I lifted his head, grabbed the seat cushion, and stuck it under his face, turning his head sideways. The bump on his forehead was red and swelling, and a little patch of skin dangled down toward his eye. Crouching, balancing, I inched around him, then sat down between his legs. I grabbed the oars.

The wind had pushed us northeast, away from the cottage shore. I'd never make it back there like this. I'd have to head for the island. Waves were slapping high on the sides of the boat, and the rain was so heavy the island was barely visible, except when lightning lit up the sky. The pelting drops stung my eyes. My jeans clung cold and wet to my thighs. All my life, my mom had told me, "Storms blow in fast over the water," but I'd never have believed one could come as fast as this. I rowed like I'd never rowed before, the little boat rocking, the wind and the rain cutting through my T-shirt. The wind was pushing us in the right direction, but I'd have to cut to the south soon. If I wasn't careful we'd be blown right past the island. I kept looking down at Tom, willing him to move, but he lay still. I brought us in right about where I'd anchored the day I explored. Somehow I got Tom's foot free from the rope and dropped the anchor in the shallow water. I jumped from the boat and waded around to the side. "Tom," I urged, putting my hand on his shoulder. "Tom, wake up!"

What was I going to do? I couldn't stand there in the water, not with lightning all around. I couldn't lift Tom, and I couldn't leave him there. Was he dead? He couldn't be. Not from just a fall. But what if the fall had made him have a heart attack or something? I was starting to panic when I thought I saw his arm move a little. I shook his shoulder. "Tom?" He groaned, and that groan was the best sound I'd ever heard. He wasn't dead! Slowly he moved, slowly he turned on his side. He propped himself up on his elbow and looked up at me.

"Are you all right?" I asked anxiously.

"No," he said. "My head hurts like hell. But I'm alive. Just give me a minute."

I stood in the water, watching him. The rain had soaked

us through. The weight of wet denim pulled at my jeans until the waistband dug into my hips, and my T-shirt was plastered to my back. Tom looked even worse than I imagined I did. He was wearing overalls, and they sagged around his middle. His long-sleeved blue shirt, the kind he always wore no matter the weather, looked almost black, it was so wet. He had a purplish, reddish knot on his forehead, but only a trickle of blood running down his cheek, so I figured the scrape wasn't too deep.

It wasn't easy to get him upright. I helped him scoot backward so he could get his legs off the seat. Then by grabbing hold of the side, he maneuvered himself around until he was able to stand.

"Can you walk?" I asked.

"I can walk," he said grimly. "Can't do this old fisherman in." He stepped out into the water, began wading to shore. "Follow me!" he yelled, over a clap of thunder, and I did.

He pushed his way through the bushes and around trees as if he knew right where he was going. In a couple of minutes, I had a suspicion. In a couple more, I was sure. He was heading for the cabin. He'd known it was there all along.

CHAPTER EIGHTEEN

WE STUMBLED THROUGH THE cabin door, and Tom barred it shut against the wind. Once inside, we just stood there panting, hearing the rain drumming on the roof, the wind whistling in the trees, and over and over again, the rumble of thunder.

"That was close," Tom said, and a grin stretched over his face. "But exciting. You look like a drowned rat, Kyle."

"What do you think you look like?" I joked back. "For starters, you have a bump the size of a baseball on your forehead."

He felt his head gingerly. "I can feel it." He walked over to the crates along the wall, and it was good to see that he seemed steady on his feet. For the first time since the rain started, I relaxed a little. Tom got busy digging into one of the crates. "Here's what we need," he told me.

He brought out some matches and a couple candles. Then he set one of the empty cans upside down on the floor. He lit a candle and held it at an angle over the can. When the melting wax formed a warm puddle on top of the can, he plunked the candle down into the hot wax and held it firmly till he was sure it was secure. "Learned that in Boy Scouts," he said.

I must have looked surprised, because he asked, "What's the matter? You think they didn't have Boy Scouts when I was young?"

I had thought that, but I wasn't going to admit it, so I just shrugged. I watched him light two more candles. In the flickering light, the cabin seemed cozy, somehow, even cheerful, and the sounds of the storm less threatening. "Pretty cool," I told him.

"Careful not to knock them over, now," he warned. "Last thing we need's a fire."

He got back to his feet and looked down at his sagging overalls. "Ought to have a change of clothes here," he said, kind of talking to himself. "Should have thought of that."

He looked closely at me then and asked, "You cold? Want to wrap up in the blanket?"

"No, I'm not cold," I lied. "You use it." He didn't reply,

just sank down on the cot, like he was exhausted. I'd never thought of him as an old man, but suddenly I realized that he was. I hoped he was going to be all right and not have a stroke on me or something like that.

"Why didn't you say the cabin was yours when I was asking about the island?" I asked, to get him talking more than anything else.

"You didn't ask me about it. You asked if anyone'd ever lived on the island, and I answered you true. The cabin's just a kind of a getaway, not a real house. When my daughter, Lou, was in school, she was always having a bunch of friends come up and stay at the house. Sometimes they'd stay for a week or so. All that chattering and giggling like to have drove me out of my mind. So I built the cabin, and now and then I'd come out here for a little bit of peace and quiet."

I didn't answer. I was busy trying to imagine Tom as the father of a teenager. Funny, even when Mom was talking about growing up near the Butlers, I'd just sort of pictured Tom as being like he was now. But he'd probably have been a good father. He'd be hard to please, but when he thought you'd done well, he'd let you know it. He might not say anything, but you'd know by the way he looked at you that he was proud, and that would be worth working for.

I wandered over to the window and looked out. The

rain was still streaming down, and the lightning was still flashing. "Looks like we're here for a while," I said. "I hope Mom's not worried."

"I hope not, too." He stood up, grunting a little, and moved over to the wall. "Well, now," he said. "Let's see what there is to eat." To eat? How could he want to eat now? He'd had bologna sandwiches and Fritos and Little Debbies on the boat. And two cans of pop.

I watched him pull out the can opener from the open box, then move over to another crate. "I think . . ." he murmured to himself. "Yep! Here it is. Baked beans. Ever eat baked beans straight from the can, Kyle? Not bad."

He turned to look at me, and he must not have liked what he saw.

"Now, listen here," he said, slamming the can down on the crate lid. "I'm getting mighty tired of you looking at me like I'm a freak or something every time I have a little bite to eat.

"Let me tell you something, boy. I made myself a promise in nineteen forty-five, the day I got out of that POW camp. Three years I'd been there. Shot down March twenty-first, nineteen forty-two."

He lifted his head and seemed to be staring at something I couldn't see. The pain on his face was something I'd never seen before and never wanted to see again. He went on, his voice lower, like he was talking to himself. "Nothing to eat but watery soup once a day. Maggots in the soup sometimes. So hungry I'd eat it anyway. The day they liberated us, I got weighed. Eighty pounds. I'd weighed a hundred seventy-five going in.

"When I got out, when I first got food, I couldn't eat it. Stomach cramps, diarrhea. But the docs took care of us, and one day I could eat again. I promised myself I'd never go hungry again, and I'm keeping that promise. When I feel like eating, I do. And I'm not about to change my ways just because some young know-it-all thinks I should."

He glared at me, and I guess my face was all shades of red. I watched him fiddle with the can opener. "I'm sorry," I said, kind of low. "I didn't know."

"Mostly we don't know, about other people," he answered, his voice gentler. For some reason I thought of Mom, crying on the steps because of selling the cottage. I hadn't even known about her, had I?

"I'm having some baked beans," he said now. "Here if you want 'em."

We must have looked a sight, each of us wetter than the other, squatting over a can of baked beans, two forks going lickety-split. But I'll have to say, those cold baked beans

162

tasted extra good. So did the fruit cocktail we had afterward.

When we'd finished, it seemed to me the rain was letting up a little. Tom seemed to think so, too. He stood in the middle of the floor, looking all around. "Pretty good job, if I do say so myself. Not a leak, after all these years."

"It's awesome," I said. "I thought about staying out here some night—when I didn't know it was yours, that is."

"You want to stay, that's all right with me. Maybe bring along your brother for company. That'd be quite an adventure for him."

"I'll say."

Just when I was feeling comfortable again with Tom, he clammed up. Neither of us said anything for maybe fifteen minutes. I wondered if he was thinking about the war, and I looked at him, trying to imagine how he might have looked weighing eighty pounds. I couldn't. There was too much of him that'd have to disappear.

Finally, he spoke. "I think it's let up enough now for us to start back. Your mom is like to be worried sick."

"Maybe she thinks I'm waiting out the rain at your cottage. She may not be worried at all."

"She's a mother. She'll be worried."

* * *

It's just as well my clothes hadn't begun to dry, because

163

brushing through the bushes and brambles would have soaked them again anyway. I marveled at how Tom seemed to know right where he was going all the time. Without my compass I'd have been lost, but he strode out purposefully, and as far as I could tell, we made a straight line to the boat.

It had about an inch of water in it, so we used the empty cans to bail it out a little. By the time we finished that, the rain had trailed off to a drizzle, and the sky was beginning to lighten. The air had the freshness that comes after a good, hard rain, and birds were beginning to sing again.

We didn't speak until we docked in front of his cottage. "Thanks, Tom," I said. I wasn't quite sure what I was thanking him for, but I felt thanks were due.

"If you decide to sleep over on the island some night," he said. "Let me know. I've got a portable radio you might want to take along."

We said good-bye, and I hurried back to the cottage, where I found everyone playing a game of Parcheesi. Mom looked up as I came in, "You're soaked!" she said. "Weren't you down at Tom's during the storm?"

"Actually," I said, "we were on the island."

It was kind of fun seeing their startled faces, and it was lots of fun telling them all about the cabin. (I hurried over the storm part, and I didn't mention Tom's fall at all. There are some things it's better for moms not to know.)

"You bum," said Andrea, "not to tell us before."

"Well, you and Vicki have your secrets, so I can have mine," I said, only half-joking.

"But that's—oh, never mind."

Of course, when I told the part about Tom suggesting Josh stay on the island with me, Josh wanted to do it that very night. He kept pestering Mom until finally she said, "If I hear one more word, you won't go at all." That silenced him, but all the rest of the day he hung around me, offering to do things for me or to bring me things. He was going to be sure he stayed on my good side.

That afternoon, while Vicki and Andrea and I were playing rummy on the porch, we heard a knock on the kitchen door.

"Tom, come in!" Mom called. The screen door scraped, and Mom exclaimed, "What happened to your head? What a goose egg! Does it hurt?"

There was a pause. I held my breath—what would he tell her? Then Tom answered, "Gave myself a good bump, didn't I? Kyle tell you about the storm, Dorrie?"

"A little. Mostly he wanted to tell us about the cabin."

"Well, I owe you an apology. I know better than to let

myself get caught on the water like that. You trusted me with your boy, Dorrie, and I let you down."

"You're both here, aren't you?" Mom said. "You made it home okay."

"Oh, but I didn't—"

I dropped my cards on the table and pushed my chair back as noisily as I could. "Tom," I called, crossing to the window between the porch and the kitchen, "tell her about that bluegill you caught!"

Tom looked at me for a long minute, then shook his head and grinned. He turned back to Mom. "It was a whopper, Dorrie! Didn't know we had any that big left in the lake."

They started talking fishing, and I went back to the card table and picked up my hand again.

Andrea looked at me. She smiled wickedly and whispered, "Pretty soon you're going to tell us the part you don't want Mom to know, aren't you, Kyle?"

And of course I did.

"I was asleep before my head hit the pillow"—Mom used to say that to show she'd been really tired, and I always thought it was an exaggeration. But if it was ever true, it was true of me that night. I just had time to picture the cabin filled with candlelight, and I was gone.

CHAPTER NINETEEN

"FLASHLIGHT."

"Check."

"Mosquito spray."

"Check."

"TP."

"Check."

Josh and I were on the porch, going over our list of supplies to take down to the boat. He liked saying "check" and shifting around the things I read off. This was the day—tonight we'd sleep on the island! Josh was so excited he could hardly stand it—too excited, maybe.

"That's all, now, isn't it, Kyle? Now can we go?" He must have asked this a million times already.

"I still gotta—" I broke off, puzzled, as I heard the crunch of gravel out back. As far as I knew, we weren't expecting anyone. A car door slammed. Josh's face lit up, and he banged out the screen door so hard I thought the hinges would break. I followed at my own pace. I knew what he was thinking, was hoping, knew he couldn't be right, but still . . .

"Hi, Josh! Your mom home?" Not Dad's voice. Mr. Barach's.

"She's in the kitchen," Josh said. "Hi, Zach!"

I guess selling a house, even a cottage, is pretty complicated. The Barachs had been stopping by with questions so often that Josh and their little boy, Zachary, had gotten to be kind of friendly. "Can I go down to the lake, please, Dad?" Zach asked now, already inching toward Josh.

"Sure, go on down. Stay with Josh, though."

"Want to see my cricket cage?" Josh offered. In a minute the two were pounding down the steps. There went my help. I thought about calling Josh back, but then I thought again. It was probably fun for him to have someone younger to show off to. I went back to the list. I didn't want to get out to the island and have to turn around and come back for something.

I could hear the low voices of Mr. Barach and Mom in the kitchen and, pretty soon, the thumping of the soccer ball down by the lake. Josh and Zach hadn't spent much time looking at the cricket cage, I noted. Maybe I'd go get Tom's radio while Josh was busy, then I could—

168

"I can get it! I can get it!" Zach's voice was shrill and excited. Footsteps on the pier, then a thud, a splash.

"Zach!" Josh's voice was frightened. "Kyle, come help!"

I was out the door and down the steps before I knew it. But at the bottom, I stopped. Zach was only chest deep in the water. He held a dripping soccer ball high above his head as he waded to shore.

"Zach! Get up here! Your mom's going to kill me." Mr. Barach must have heard the commotion. He was standing outside the porch door. I couldn't tell if his voice sounded more angry or afraid. Zach handed the ball to Josh and dripped past me up the steps.

"Did you kick that ball?" I asked Josh. I didn't give him time to answer. "How many times have we told you—you don't kick down here, you dribble! Do you realize what might have happened if Zach'd fallen in over his head? You don't even know if he can swim." I took a deep breath, and then I added coldly, "If you can't follow directions any better than that, you're not old enough for a night on the island." Okay, so I was a little rough. I didn't really plan to leave him behind, but I figured it wouldn't hurt to let him think that for a while.

Josh had been trying to interrupt, but now he clamped his mouth shut. He stared at me, his eyes big. Then he turned and went up the steps, his head hanging, his footsteps slow. I waited till I saw him at the cottage door. He stood there for a minute, watching Mr. Barach squat on the walk and hug Zach tightly. I was almost to the top when Josh saw me coming. He turned away and went inside. I hung around while Mom got a beach towel to wrap Zach in and saw both Barachs off. I told her I was going down to get Tom's radio. I'd talk to Josh when I got back. Let him stew until then.

* * *

No one was in the cottage when I got back an hour or so later with Tom's radio under my arm. I was grabbing a snack when Mom came through the kitchen door. She caught me just taking the milk bottle away from my lips, but she didn't even notice.

Her face was shining again. Dad had called, I guessed. Sure enough—"I just talked to your father, Kyle. He's had the best news!"

"He's found a new hole to hide in?" I asked sarcastically.

She ignored me. "He's sold a book, Kyle! Isn't that great? He says it's something completely different for him. And he wanted to be sure I told you the title."

"Confessions of a Missing Father?" The sarcasm was automatic—I couldn't help it.

"Don't get smart. It's called *Isabel and Ike Go Fishing*. And he said, 'Tell Kyle I said thanks for the advice.' You gave him advice, Kyle?"

Huh. I guess he did read my letter. "I might have said something back when I cared what he did," I told her.

Mom broke into my thoughts. "Where's Josh, Kyle? I was looking for him when I got the telephone call. Was he with you?"

"Nope. I thought he was in here. Maybe he's with Andrea and Vicki, wherever they are."

"Playing Monopoly down at Marshalls'. He's not with them, I checked," Mom said. "And I called over and over, and I rang Mom's bell twice. Then I decided he must have gone down to Clyde's with you."

"Nope. Where did you look?"

"Everywhere I could think of—down by the lake first, of course. Wherever he is, he isn't hungry, because half a loaf of bread is gone, not to mention most of the peanut butter. I found the open jar with the knife still in it on the table when I came back from chatting with the new people up on the hill."

She sounded more worried than angry, so I patted her on the back. "I'll find him," I promised.

Mom said she'd looked down by the lake, so I went out

the back door. I was walking around the wagon when I noticed the inside light was on. Someone hadn't shut the door tight. I went over to check and found the glove compartment open. Josh, for sure—he never closes a drawer or a door. But what had he wanted in there?

I looked up and down the road, but I saw no sign of him. Crud! I'd wanted to leave by three. Now we'd have a late start. Why wasn't he here? Earlier, he'd been "chomping at the bit," as Gram used to say. And then I remembered. Josh wouldn't be in a hurry now, because he thought he wasn't going along. So what would he do instead? An idea struck me. "Mom," I called through the door, "is Josh's money in his box?" Josh's "treasure box" was where he stashed his lake souvenirs. It was also where he hoarded his cricket money.

In a minute she called back, "It's all gone, Kyle."

"He must have gone down to Clyde's," I called, and I think my relief sounded in my voice. I don't know what I'd been afraid of, but I was glad to think of a logical explanation for Josh's absence. Of course, he should have told Mom that's what he was going to do, but I don't think anyone had explicitly said he couldn't leave the cottage area without permission. And if no one had, Josh would be sure to point that out. He always obeyed the letter of the law. We all thought he'd be a lawyer when he grew up—a defense lawyer. I opened the back screen door and stuck my head inside. "I'll go check," I said.

I started down the road. I was getting mad now. Just as I got to Tom's, he came out of his door, car keys in hand. "Going into Cass," he said. "Thought you and Josh would be off by now."

"I gotta find Josh first. I think he may have gone to Clyde's for some dumb reason. He didn't tell Mom he was leaving, and she's all worried. He's probably on the way home now."

"Hop in," Tom said. I did.

As we drove along, I kept looking for Josh. Tom was looking, too. It was nice of him to give me a ride. He didn't say anything, but whenever I looked over at him I felt kind of—I guess comforted is the best word. Strange. But we didn't see Josh, and at the bait shop Tom went in with me.

"Seen Dorrie Chester's younger boy today, Clyde?" Tom asked.

"Sure," Clyde answered, lowering his newspaper. "He was in a while ago, hauling a backpack that looked to weigh almost more'n he does. Bought a flashlight and batteries. I put it together for him, made sure it worked. I asked was you all going camping, and he allowed as you were. He ain't back yet? Should be."

Tom and I stared at each other. "He must have gone the other way," Tom said. "Why in thunder?"

I was beginning to guess. That open glove compartment . . . "Did he have a map with him?" I asked Clyde.

"Sure did, Michigan, Indiana, Ohio. He wanted me to show him where the lake is, and Cass, and—" but Tom had wheeled around as fast as a man his size could wheel, and we left Clyde in mid-sentence, staring after us.

"Josh get into a row with your mother?" Tom asked as we drove along toward the turnoff to Cassopolis.

"I don't think it was Mom," I said. "I think it was me."

"I ran away once when I was his age. Got as far as the next block. Saw some kids I knew, put down my suitcase, and joined a game of King of the Mountain. Forgot all about running away."

"I don't think Josh is running away," I said slowly. "I think he's running to."

In my mind's eye I could see him leaping up on Dad the way he always did. I saw him wrap himself around Dad's middle, rub his face against Dad's beard. That's where he was going—to Dad.

We found him a mile or so farther on, trudging along. When he heard the car motor, he glanced over his shoulder, and for a minute, I thought he was going to run off

174

into the trees and I'd have to chase him. But he didn't.

Tom drew up alongside. Josh opened the door and climbed in back. When he was settled, Tom turned around and asked him, "Which way?"

"Back to the cottage, I guess," Josh said, looking at Tom, looking out the window, looking anywhere but at me. "Is my mom mad?" he asked Tom.

Tom let me answer. "Not now. Now she's just worried. But she will be, after she sees you're back safe and sound."

No one said anything for a while. As we hit the stretch between Clyde's and the cottage, though, Josh said, "Cincinnati's a lot farther than I thought."

Tom offered to drive us all the way, but when we got to his house, I told him we'd walk from there. "You sure?" he asked.

"I'm sure," I said. "And Tom—thanks a lot."

He just grunted, but he kind of clapped me on the shoulder. I put the backpack on my own back. Clyde was right—it was super heavy. "See you," I told him.

"What were you going to do when you got to Cincinnati?" I asked Josh as we walked along.

"Call Dad."

"I thought so." He looked awfully little walking beside me. He looked—I searched my mind for the word I

175

wanted—he looked defeated. Not cocky anymore, not like himself. I couldn't take it. "Josh? You still want to spend the night on the island with me?"

I've heard about faces lighting up. This was the first time I'd ever seen it. "Can I?"

"If Mom's not too mad to let you."

He perked right up. He didn't start talking, but he straightened his shoulders and walked a little faster. I felt a surge of self-satisfaction. Being a good big brother was just a matter of knowing when to be firm and when to be soft, I thought. I was congratulating myself when Josh looked up at me.

"Kyle?"

"Yeah?"

"The ball that went in the water? I didn't kick it, Kyle. Zach did. He tried to kick it to me, and it went sideways."

"Zach kicked it? Why didn't you say?"

"I tried. You wouldn't let me talk."

His voice was matter-of-fact. He wasn't reproaching me, wasn't feeling sorry for himself, just telling it like he saw it. "I'm going to put the rest of my money back before we go. I'll wait in the cottage." He ran ahead, and his smart-ass brother, who thought he knew everything, followed along.

* * *

176

It wasn't easy to get Mom to say yes. First she grabbed Josh and hugged him, then it was all, "Where were you?" "What were you thinking?" "Haven't I told you . . . ?" "Didn't you realize . . . ?" But even when Mom is shooting questions at you, she's watching and listening and trying to understand. So in the end she gave in.

It was almost six before we left. Vicki and Andrea and Mom stood on the pier and waved as we rowed away. They stood there for a long time. I took my hand off the oar long enough to wave back. Josh didn't turn around to wave. He was looking toward the island. He looked tired. And peaceful. And happy.

CHAPTER TWENTY

IT'S HARD TO ADMIT, BUT if Josh hadn't come along, I might not have stuck it out that night. I'd thought it was dark up at the cottage at night, but in the cabin, surrounded by trees, I began to get an idea of what it must be like to be blind. And one thing's for sure—noises are a lot louder, a lot scarier, when you can't see what's causing them.

It had been fun taking Josh to the cabin. With him to help, we managed to carry all our stuff in only one trip. He followed me through the bushes, and at one point he said, "We aren't lost, are we, Kyle?" I didn't let him see me smile—the island wasn't that big. But maybe it was to a seven-year-old.

When I could see the cabin ahead I called back, "There it is—through the trees—see it?" Josh was so excited at that point he pushed past me. "Let me go first now, okay?" and he plowed ahead without waiting for an answer.

I watched him go. Weighed down by our backpack, his shoulders looked narrow and kind of stooped, but he hadn't once complained about the weight. I was carrying my sleeping bag, Tom's radio, and a laundry bag I'd stuffed with everything that hadn't fit in the backpack. I'd be glad to drop my load, too.

"Cool!" Josh said when we got to the clearing and he had his first whole view.

"Wait till you see inside."

"Maybe we can stay all week!"

I'd thought something like that myself. "Another time, maybe," I answered.

We crossed the clearing, and I unhooked the door. "It's kind of dark in here," Josh said when he stepped in.

"There's only one window. But if we leave the door open, it helps."

"Just leave it open? What if a bear walked in?"

"There aren't any bears."

But Josh was still Josh. "There could be," he said. "They could have been hiding before." I never could argue with Josh's "could's," so I let it go.

"You hungry yet?" I asked. That was a dumb question: if he'd nodded any harder, his head would've fallen off. "We'll see what Mom sent," I told him. Tom had told me to eat any of the food I wanted from the cans, but Mom was worried it might not still be good, so she and Andrea had packed us salami sandwiches. There was a bag of cookies, too. Vicki had made them that morning, and they were a little burned. Mom told her not to feel bad, that the oven wasn't very dependable. Of course, if Vick hadn't been reading, she might have noticed the burning smell, but it was like Mom not to point that out. Mom had put in carrots and celery sticks, too, but she should have known that was a waste of effort. "Maybe we should each eat one, so she won't feel bad," I said, handing Josh a carrot. (Carrots aren't so bad, but celery isn't worth the chewing.)

"Or we could feed them to the fishes on the way home," he suggested with that big smile that shows where his teeth are missing. I laughed and put them back in the lunch bag.

After dinner we had a couple of hours to get things set the way we wanted them and explore the woods around the cabin. But when it started getting dark, we were both glad to go inside and light the candles. I would have loved to build a little campfire and toast marshmallows, but I had promised Mom no fires.

We listened to Tom's radio for a while, and Josh brought out a deck of cards he'd stuck in his jeans pocket. "Good idea," I told him when he showed me, and he beamed.

"You want to play Go Fish?" he asked.

"How about if I teach you poker instead?" Dad had taught me how to play poker when I was about Josh's age, and once in a while he and Mom and us older kids had sat up playing until almost eleven. We would use the red, white, and blue chips Dad'd had since college. He never would bet for money, though. I used to try to get him to bet money on something, anything. I'd set up a situation where he couldn't lose and offer him tremendous odds, but he wouldn't even bet a quarter. "Bad habit to get into," he'd say.

I'd answered, "But it's just for fun. Just this once."

And he'd look at me all serious and answer, "Lots of people have been talked into things they regret by someone who said 'Just this once' to them, Kyle." And he wouldn't budge.

So now I only taught Josh the playing part—I figured I could teach him the betting part later. We didn't have any chips anyway. He caught on pretty well, and we played until he started to yawn. I was tired, too, I realized, and I caught myself yawning along with him. I gave him the cot and the blanket and spread my sleeping bag on the floor. Then I went over and barred the door. "Can we turn the radio off now?" Josh asked. That wasn't what I'd planned, but there wasn't anything good on, so I said, "Sure," and clicked it off.

It was very quiet then.

"Are we going to leave the candles lit?"

"Mom made me promise not to. She didn't want us sleeping with what she called 'an untended fire.' But we'll be okay."

I blew out the candles and crawled over to my sleeping bag. "'Night, Josh," I said.

"Good night. Thanks for bringing me, Kyle."

I smiled even though he couldn't see me in the dark. "I'm glad you're here."

I lay there then, listening to the night sounds outside the cabin. Just as I was beginning to get drowsy, I heard Josh ask sleepily, "How many days are there in May?"

"Thirty-one. Why?"

"I'm counting the days Dad's been gone. I miss him, don't you?" I started to say no automatically, but the word stuck in my throat. "Kyle?"

"Yeah, I miss him."

It was quiet again, and I was almost asleep when I heard, "One hundred fifty-two."

CHAPTER TWENTY-ONE

I WONDER HOW OLD YOU ARE when you quit getting
excited about birthdays. A lot older than me, I guess. It was
fun to wake up July 19 and know that now I was (un)offi-
cially a teenager. Three years and five months and I'd be
able to drive!

The early part of the day was like any other. Tom Butler
had offered to let me have the morning off if I wanted, but
I told him I'd really just as soon fish with him in the morning as do anything else. Fishing with Tom had come to be
a really—what's the best word?—companionable way to
start the day. I still didn't like the way he ate so much, but
it didn't disgust me the way it used to. I was trying to understand it, like I was trying to understand Mom's smoking, but it wasn't easy.

In the afternoon we all went swimming. Even Mom
went. For the first time, Josh swam all the way from our pier

to Marshalls' float. I swam right alongside him, naturally. When he got to the float and pulled himself up, even Jeff and Brad applauded him. Good thing he didn't have on a shirt; he would have "bust his buttons"—another Gram expression. I used to love when she said it. I'd see a mind-movie of a fat man in a plaid suit puffing out his chest, and all his buttons would come flying off and bounce around on the floor.

It was a fun afternoon. Vicki and Andrea and I splashed around and raced each other just like old times. Brad and Jeff weren't as bad as they'd been before. Around four, though, I was ready to go fishing again. To my surprise, Andrea said she wanted to go along this time, so the two of us swam lazily back to the pier. Then she went up to the cottage to get her sketchbook while I loaded up the boat.

"Want me to row?" she asked when she came down.

"Think we'll get there today if you do?" I teased.

She made a face at me and hopped into the boat. "Just watch," she said. As soon as I got settled, she grabbed the oars. There was no way I was going to get them back.

I kind of lay back on my elbows, curious to see where she would head. Like I expected, she rowed us down where the water lilies grow. "We should have flowers on the table for your birthday dinner," she told me.

When we were anchored, I threw out my line, and she settled back to sketch. Andrea's great to have along when you're fishing. If you bring one in, she'll help you net, but mostly she just sits still and looks at things. Funny, I can look at something and think I've seen it, but then Andrea will say, "Did you notice. . ." and she'll have seen something about it that I completely missed.

After a while, I glanced over at her drawing. She'd sketched a single water lily with a dragonfly poised above. Her drawings were so good!

"Did you just start that sketchbook today?" I asked.

"Mmm-hmm."

"You mean you've filled a whole sketchbook, and I haven't seen anything in it?" I decided not to mention that one page I'd seen before, when she got all mad.

"I guess so. I'll show you later."

After that, neither of us said much for a while. I fished till Mom rang the bell. As I pulled in my line, I said, "This has been a great birthday, in spite of the cottage."

She knew what I meant and nodded. Then she smiled and said, "But it's not over yet. Presents still to come, you know."

I knew, but somehow the thought of them wasn't as important as usual. It would take a fairy godmother to give me what I really wanted, I thought.

For supper we had chicken and dumplings. Mom said having chicken and dumplings in the middle of the summer was the dumbest thing she ever heard of, but on our birthdays she'll cook anything we ask for, and chicken and dumplings is my favorite.

All during the meal Andrea and Vicki were giggling and whispering, but this time I didn't mind. I knew they were trying to get me curious about something, so I just pretended not to notice.

When we'd finished the chicken and dumplings, which were great, Andrea and Vicki cleared the table, and Mom brought out the cake. It was from the bakery in Cassopolis, because Mom said she didn't trust the oven after Vicki's cookies got burned. I didn't care. It was chocolate, and that was enough.

Everyone was singing "Happy Birthday" and I was blowing out the candles when Tom Butler knocked at the door and walked in.

"Sit down, Tom. I'm glad you could make it," Mom said.

"Never turn down a chance to eat birthday cake," he answered.

For the next half hour, we laughed and talked and talked and laughed until Mom said, "Well, if everyone's finished, I guess it's present time."

She was about to move the leftover cake to the countertop when I happened to look at Tom. He was watching her pick up the platter, and the look on his face was more than I could take. "Cut Tom another piece first," I told Mom. So what if he'd already eaten more than anyone else—he could have worse faults, I guess.

Now Josh said, "Open my present first, Kyle, please!"

He handed me a large wrapped package. It was thin and light, with an odd shape.

"Thanks, Josh," I told him.

"You haven't seen it yet! You're going to like it, I bet."

I pulled off the paper and there was a plywood poster in the shape of a fish. It had a picture of a fisherman with his arms stretched out, and underneath was a poem called "Fisherman's Prayer":

> Lord, give me grace to catch a fish
> So big that even I
> When telling of it afterwards
> May never need to lie.

I laughed. "It's a great present, Josh. Thanks."

"Mom next," said Vicki.

Mom handed me two packages. One was a book, I

knew, because we always get a book from her for our birthdays. I opened it first. A thick, grown-up-looking volume was in my hands. *"The Compleat Angler, or The Contemplative Man's Recreation,* by Izaak Walton," I read. "Hey, that's not how you spell *complete.*"

"That's the way they spelled it in the 1600s," Mom said. "That's when it was written. It's a classic. I hope you'll enjoy it." She looked anxious, the way she always does when she gives us a book.

"I'll probably never even read it," I told her with a grin. I love to tease Mom. My second present from her was my own tackle box.

I stared at it with a lump in my throat. I didn't say anything.

"Don't you like it?" she asked.

"It's great," I said. "Just the kind I wanted. Only, where will I use it?"

I didn't mean to be ungrateful. It just hit me, and the words came out of my mouth before I knew they were going to.

There was an awkward silence, and then Andrea jumped up. "Now, ours!" she said—in such a hurry to smooth things over that she practically shoved a package under my nose. "This is from Vicki and me."

I wasn't having fun anymore. What I wanted to do was leave the kitchen and go sit out on the pier in the dark all by myself on my last birthday here. But I tried to look eager as I unwrapped the package. Out of the corner of my eye, I saw Vicki grab Andrea's hand—whatever it was, the two of them were sure excited about it.

Inside was a sketchbook. I stared at it, puzzled. Why would I want a sketchbook? I opened it slowly, and there on the first page was a drawing of the cottage. It was beautiful. It looked just right, down to the shadows on the steps. Underneath, in Vicki's calligraphy, it said, "For Kyle, who loved it best."

"Turn the page," Josh urged.

I turned page after page. Each one had a sketch of something I knew and loved. The pump, the roll-away with Vicki lying on it, reading. Mom sitting at the kitchen table with a cup of coffee in front of her, the glass with the wildflowers Vicki had picked. And underneath each sketch Vicki had penned a caption or comment.

"You guys . . ." I said. I couldn't say anything more.

"Now you know why I wouldn't let you see my sketchbook," Andrea said.

"And why we were always whispering," Vicki added.

Even though I was thirteen, I gave everyone a hug.

189

When I got to Tom I hesitated, I guess, because he laughed and pushed back his chair. He got to his feet, saying, "It's okay to give another man a hug, Kyle. Long as you thump him on the back at the same time," so we hugged and thumped each other, and then he sat back down and looked at Mom. "Time for you to tell him, Dorrie."

I looked at Mom, too. She had a big smile. "Tom is offering you the chance to spend next summer with him in his cottage, Kyle. Free room and board, and all you need do in exchange is fish with him in the mornings. Not only that, but he's said the rest of us can spend a few weeks there, too, if we like."

Everyone was looking at me, waiting for me to say something. But I couldn't. If I tried to talk I'd cry. All I could think was, I don't have to say good-bye for good! I get to come back!

"Course, if you're not interested . . ." Tom teased.

That was enough to snap me out of it. I smiled so wide I thought my face would break. "You bet I'm interested! I'm just having trouble believing it."

"Not such a big deal. I need your help."

"Thanks, Tom. It's so—it's—just thanks."

A knock at the door surprised us all. Mrs. Morley stuck her head in. "Happy Birthday, Kyle. Call for you over at our house. Your dad wants to know will you come talk to him?"

I looked at Mom. She looked back at me with pleading eyes. I looked at Tom and remembered what he'd said: "Mostly we don't know, about other people." And Vicki and Andrea—I'd been mad at them for shutting me out, when all the time they'd been planning for my birthday. Then I looked at Josh. He looked steadily back at me, and I realized I hadn't the slightest idea what he was thinking. I just didn't know. Maybe there were things I didn't know about Dad? "All right, Mrs. Morley," I said. "I'll talk to him. Come on, Josh. You can talk after."